Ink & Dust

Silky Ink
Book 1

Khloe Wren

ISBN ebook: 978-1-922942-01-2
ISBN print: 978-1-922942-00-5

Cover Credits:
Model: Michelle McLeod
Photographer: Jean Woodfin of JW Photography &
Covers
Digital Artist: Khloe Wren

Editing Credits:
Editors: Carolyn Depew of Write Right Edits
Rainy Kaye

Books by Khloe Wren

Charon MC:

Inking Eagle

Fighting Mac

Chasing Taz

Claiming Tiny

Saving Scout

Tripping Nitro

Scout's Legacy

Mac's Destiny

Losing Bash

Finding Needles

Forging Blade

Taming Keys

Breaking Arrow

Taz's Guards

Shielding Bank

Fire and Snow:

Guardian's Heart

Noble Guardian

Guardian's Shadow

Fierce Guardian

Necessary Alpha

Protective Instincts

Jaguar Secrets:

FireStarter

Other Titles:

Fireworks

Scarred Perfection

Scandals: Zeck

Mirror Image Seduction

The Warrior, The Witch & The Wombat

Deception

Kings of Sydney: Daniil

Biography

Khloe Wren lives in rural South Australia with her husband, two daughters and an ever changing list of animals!

She started writing in 2013 and has published over 40 books since then in the romantic suspense genre. She writes both paranormal and contemporary stories, including her best selling series Charon MC.

Khloe enjoys writing outside of the box and she loves her heroes strong, and her heroines even stronger.

facebook.com/khloe.wren.3

instagram.com/khloewren

bookbub.com/authors/khloewren

Acknowledgments

I've never taken as long to write a book as I have with this one. It's been around three or four years since I first planned Ink & Dust. Every time I attempted to work on it, I wouldn't get far before the story would stall so I'd move onto other projects. So I'm quite sure many people close to me, especially my husband, are very grateful I've finally finished writing this book so I'll stop lamenting to them about not having it done!

So, with that, I give an extra thanks to my husband and kids for not smothering me in my sleep over the past few years. I know there have probably been times you've all considered it.

Massive thanks to Jo-Carol, Stacey and Brent for all your help on this one. Many, many conversations have been had over the years. To Jena McCormick, your knowledge from working with rescued horses was a huge help. I know I also had many chats with a rancher that was a friend of a friend, but I didn't add his name to my note file and now I can't find it! But his willingness to answer all my cattle/ranch questions was invaluable to getting this story done.

To Carolyn, not only did you work miracles to edit this one in a rush for me, but your horse knowledge was invaluable. Also thanks to Rainy, for your assistance in helping me work out why this story had stalled out.

Thanks to Seven and the crew at Ink Couture in New York for your advice on tattooing and for designing the awesome series logo.

I'm sure I'm missing many, many people who have helped me over the years with this one as I seem to have lost a note file where I was keeping a list of everyone somewhere along the way.

Finally, an acknowledgement of the images you'll find on the back cover of the print version of each book in this series. Claudia Bost was one of my closest friends, we lived half a world apart and didn't get to see each other often, but we chatted online regularly. Back in 2019, before the world went mad, we were both in New York for an event and we did a photo shoot in the Ink Couture shop with Chelle, Al and Seven. The images didn't end up being quite right for the covers, but I loved them enough I've worked them into the back covers to honor my friend who we lost a couple of months ago to cancer.

xo
Khloe

SILKY INK
TX

Chapter One

Saturday 20 Jan 2018

Gabs

I'D NEVER FOUND anything that soothed and calmed me like riding a horse. Whenever I had more than an hour free, I was here with my landlord's horses. John was happy for me to ride his mares whenever I wanted to, as long as I helped take care of them, which I was more than happy to do. Any excuse to spend more time around these gorgeous animals, I was there.

With a grin, I gave Whiskey a nudge and she sped up into a canter, taking us flying over the trail we were following. Inhaling the fresh air deep into my lungs, I instantly felt lighter. All my troubles floated away with the wind that rushed past my face.

By the time I rode Whiskey up the driveway toward the barn, I was calm and more than ready to face another day of my busy life. At least, I was until I saw the ATV parked outside the building. Whiskey stiffened beneath me, and I reached out to stroke the side of her neck.

"Shh, it's all right, girl. Ain't nothing for you to worry about."

Nope. The man I knew who was waiting for me was no threat to the horses. Realizing there was nothing I could do to avoid Royce, my landlord's adult son, I kept Whiskey moving until we were in front of the barn. Dismounting, I led her through the open door and into the aisle.

"Hey, Gabriela, have a nice ride?"

Like it always had, Royce's nasally voice sent a shudder running through me. He'd been trying to get into my panties since we were in our teens. He'd always been creepy as hell, and I hadn't wanted anything to do with him—then or now. Due to the fact that our parents went to the same church, I'd had to see him way too regularly when I was younger. It was a huge relief when he'd moved away as soon as he graduated college. Even though the little trailer I currently rented from his parents sat on the corner of their ranch, I hadn't had to deal with him.

That had changed earlier this month when he reappeared like the prodigal son, expecting everyone to be overjoyed at his return. It sure as hell wasn't joy that I felt. Nope. Especially since he'd taken over running the barn, which included overseeing how I performed chores. I mentally rolled my eyes. Like I needed damn supervision. I'd lived in that trailer for nearly two years now and had been working with these horses that entire time. Sure, in the beginning John had been there each day to help and teach me, but it hadn't taken long for him to see that I was a natural with the big animals and had a good memory. After that, he'd been content to only pop in occasionally to catch up with me when I was here. He still used them for ranch work, checking the cattle and such, but since he had three horses, there were always at least two here no matter what time I came over.

Giving him a fake smile, I dug deep to remain polite to the slimeball. "It's a lovely day. You should get out and enjoy it."

Since I didn't have to go into Silky Ink tonight, I'd left it until later in the afternoon to come over. The air was just turning crisp, but it wouldn't get dark for a while yet, so definitely not too late to go out for a ride. I'd much rather he not be around while I finished a few chores before I left, starting with grooming Whiskey, then feeding and watering all three horses. But I knew he wouldn't go. Not only did he never ride, but I'd also noticed the way he'd flinched whenever one of the mares moved too close to him.

I mentally shook my head. How could anyone not like these gentle animals? Even if he hadn't been sleazy as hell and constantly under my feet whenever I was here in the barn slowing me down, I would have never given him the time of day because of how the horses reacted to him. Animals knew things we didn't, and I trusted that.

Basically, even if hell froze over, I wouldn't go out with the asshole. But he never seemed to get the message.

"Nah, you know me. I'll stick with the ATV. Easier than a horse. You simply start it up and go, then just park it when you're done."

He said that like it was a good thing. I ran my palm over Whiskey's neck to help calm her before I reached for the curry to start brushing her. As always, I did my best to ignore Royce as I fed and watered the mares. As I was finishing up, he stepped directly into my path, forcing me to stop and focus on him.

"How long are you going to ignore this thing between us, Gabriela?"

Holding in a cringe at him using my full name again, I slammed my hands on my hips and glared straight into his eyes.

"There's nothing to ignore, Royce. There never has nor will there ever be anything between us. You really need to accept that and move on."

Anger flashed over his face a moment before it settled back into a smirk. Both expressions had me frowning at what he might do next.

"Only reason you're allowed to come ride our horses is because I permit it. And I know you're only here so you can see me. If you don't want to have a relationship with me? Well, there's no reason for you to be here now, is there?"

Shock had me stumbling back a step before I could stop myself.

"I'm here because I help your father look after the horses. He knows how much I've always loved them, so offered to trade chores for saddle time."

"Well, now you can pay in other ways." He reached out toward my arm, but I jerked away before he could get hold of me.

"Don't you dare touch me. And I'm not ever going to sleep with you! I'm going to go up to the house to see your dad. There's no way he'd allow you to pull this shit."

I went to move around him, but he stepped into my path again, forcing me to either stop or physically push past him. Since I didn't want to touch him at all, I stopped and growled, "Let me by."

He shook his head and fear crept up my spine.

"No. If you want to keep coming over to ride, you're going to need to do exactly what I tell you to do."

Was this really happening? Royce may have always given off a creepy vibe, but he'd never actually directly threatened me before.

"Where's your dad? He's the one I made the deal with, so he's the only one who can change the terms."

With his reedy arms folded over his chest, he ran his gaze up and down my body.

"Dad's not well, so he's handed over control of the ranch to me. His only son. Everything on this property is mine to do with as I choose."

I clenched my fists, tempted to throw a punch at the bastard but knowing it wouldn't do me a lick of good. Nor would it help John if he was truly sick.

Nearly vibrating with my rage, I stormed past him, shoving his arm away when he tried to grab me. A knee to his gut took him out of my path. Winded, he dropped to the ground.

"I'm going up to see your folks. If they're really sick, they're going to need care."

By the time I was out of the barn and walking up the path to the house, he stumbled out behind me.

"One more step and I'll call the sheriff and have you charged with trespassing and assault. You're not welcome on the property anymore, Gabriela. You need to leave."

Panic shook me to my core, making me spin on him.

"I've lived in my trailer for years, Royce. I have a legal lease signed by your father and me. You can't just kick me out of my own damn home."

He struggled to stand straight, one arm wrapped around his middle. "Fine. You're allowed on the land around your trailer, but not anywhere else on the property. And you're not allowed near the fucking horses."

Tears pricked my eyes, but I held them in. I would not let Royce see me cry. And I didn't want to risk him lashing out further and forcing me out of my home.

With my head held high, I changed direction, back toward my trailer. I climbed over the fence to walk across the pasture back to my home. The one I hoped I wouldn't have to leave soon.

Gabs

Even after a hot shower I was still on edge, angry and upset over what had happened with Royce. Looking around my small trailer, I couldn't help but wonder if I was going to have to move soon. This place wasn't much, but it was mine. And it had allowed me the chance to work with horses even though I couldn't afford one of my own yet.

When tears stung the backs of my eyes again, I cursed under my breath before I headed back to my bedroom to shower and get changed. No way could I stay in tonight. I would only get myself worked up and end up an emotional mess.

As I dressed to head out, I contemplated where to go. If I went to the bar, Styx, in town, I would be surrounded by members of the local motorcycle club, the Charon MC. Normally, that wouldn't bother me, but tonight I was too on edge, and they'd notice. Then one of them would call Silk and she'd be there in my face, demanding to know what was going on. Or not. And that would truly crush me.

Silk had been my best friend since we were twelve years old. We'd gone through so many of life's ups and downs together, including planning out our entire futures. Standing beside her as we opened Silky Ink four years ago had been a dream come true for us both. It was officially her shop and her name on the window, but that was because she'd had the capital to set it up and I hadn't, nor had I wanted to go into debt just so my name would be in the mix. I was happy for Silk, proud to be working there, living our teenage dream together.

But over the last year or so, things had changed. She'd met her man, Eagle, and he'd taken all her attention. Silky Ink wasn't her top priority anymore, nor did she have time for her bestie. It wasn't just Eagle who took up her time, she now had a beautiful baby boy to occupy her. Some days, I wondered if she even remembered I was alive.

Shaking my head, I tried to shrug off the self-pity party. That thinking wasn't fair to my lifelong friend. I was honestly happy for her. She owned a successful business, had a loving husband, and an adorable son. Her life was complete, and the problem was I wished mine was too. The fact I didn't have a massive circle of friends hadn't really mattered when I'd lived with Silk, and we were both single. Not having a significant other hadn't bothered me when I'd been able to talk to her twenty-four/seven about anything, been able to get a hug when I needed one. When we'd both been doing the single lady thing together.

With a growl, I dashed away the tears that had slipped free. Returning to the bathroom, I splashed water on my face and put on a little makeup. With the way my emotions were spiraling, tonight was not the time to touch that whole mess with Silk. Nor did I want to pull her away from her new family this late in the day. No doubt she was feeding her son or getting him to bed. She didn't need to add dealing with my shit on top of that, which meant heading into Bridgewater was out.

I just wanted to go somewhere for a few drinks, to relax and forget my troubles with no pressure to explain a damn thing.

As I pulled a brush through my long, straight, silver hair, I remembered seeing fliers for a live band that was playing tonight at The Barn, a small honky tonk about a half an hour's drive north. Right now, that sounded perfect. I'd be able to have a few drinks, get some food and listen to the band for a while, then I'd drive myself home and climb into bed. I'd worry about Royce and his bullshit tomorrow.

Happy with my new plan, I finished getting ready all the while hoping like hell nothing else would crop up and ruin my night further.

Gabs

It didn't take long for my simple plan to turn to shit. Less than a minute after I sat down at a tall table with my first shot of whiskey and a glass of soda, two wannabe cowboys came my way. As they approached, I downed my shot and tried to focus on the burn rather than their leering stares.

One of them leaned onto the table with a grin so creepy it had a shiver running down my spine. Royce had nothing on this guy. "Hey, there, pretty lady, tell me whatchya drinkin' and I'll get you another one."

Like I would ever touch a damn thing this man gave me. I flipped my tongue ring over the roof of my mouth for a moment before I responded.

"Sorry, fellas, but I'm not looking for drinking buddies tonight."

The other man moved in closer, like he was going to have better luck. He'd obviously tried a little harder than his buddy to look the part. He wore a crinkled-up, straw imitation cowboy hat on his head and a big 'ol belt buckle he'd no doubt picked up at a tourist shop. Because I highly doubted this guy had ever even ridden a horse, let alone competed in a rodeo.

"You like my buckle, bunny? More than happy to show you how well I rode to win it."

The way he thrust his hips like he thought he was Elvis or some shit had me rolling my eyes. Could these men be any more cliché? I had to wonder if these bullshit lines of theirs ever worked. A girl would have to be hella desperate.

After taking a sip from my soda, I ran my gaze over the one who'd spoken.

"Let me guess… you'll last the whole eight seconds."

His buddy choked on a laugh until the one who'd spoken turned on him with a frown. Before either one could say another word, I slipped from the table, leaving my half empty soda behind. This situation could rapidly turn ugly, and it was simply easier for me to move along.

"I suggest you go find some other lady to focus your attention on. I'm not interested."

With that, I turned away and headed to the bathroom. I hoped once I was out of sight, they'd move on to bother someone else.

Seemed all my plans were going to shit

tonight because when I came out, they were waiting for me in the dimly lit hallway.

The one who'd tried to buy me a drink spoke up. "We weren't done talking when you walked away, sweets. That was just plain rude. Don't you think, Bob?"

"Yeah, Billy. Downright hurt my feelings."

I rolled my eyes again. I was being accosted by Billy and Bob. For real. I couldn't make this shit up. With a shake of my head, I went to move past them, praying they were all hat and no cattle.

Strong arms wrapped around me from behind, pinning me against Bob's front. Bile rose up my throat as his erection pressed against my ass, but I refused to show these two any fear. And after already having dealt with Royce's bullshit, I was not in the mood to tolerate any from these two bastards.

I would not go quietly to the slaughter. I might look all sweet and harmless, but I wasn't completely without defenses. Mac, one of the newer members of the Charon MC, had started self-defense classes for women a year or so ago at the local gym. I'd gone to a few of them, feeling better that I might be able to defend myself should something like this ever happen. It was looking like I'd get to test out what I'd learned tonight.

Deciding that if I could attract some

attention from those out in the main bar area, these two creeps might decide I was more trouble than I was worth. I parted my lips to scream but before any sound came out, Billy slammed his hand over my mouth.

"Don't go making this harder that it has to be, sweets. Come willingly and we'll let you have a little fun too."

My gut churned at what they intended to do, while my eyes stung from the stench of his breath. Refusing to panic, I forced my mind to calm as I took in everything I could about my attackers. Bob was still behind me, restraining me, and since I could feel his breath moving my hair, I knew he was close enough for me to head-butt if I was quick enough. Then, if I could land a kick to Billy's groin before he realized what I was doing, I might be able to break free and run the hell away from the pair of them. But I couldn't do any of that while Billy's hand was pressed tightly against my mouth.

When a plan formed in my mind on how to get him to release his grip, hope bloomed inside me. I just might have a chance at getting out of this. Considering the alternative was to let these two drag me out through the back exit so they could do their worst, anything was worth a shot at this point.

Quickly, I opened my mouth until I could

take some of his flesh between my teeth, then I bit down. Hard. I was careful to not break his skin. I had no clue what a creep like this would have running in his veins, but I knew I didn't want it in me.

When Billy pulled away with a curse, I threw my head back, ignoring the flare of pain as I connected with Bob's face. A grin stretched my lips at the satisfying crunch of bone that I hoped was the asshole's nose breaking. Bob released me but before I could kick out at Billy, he back-handed me across the face with enough force it spun me into the wall. Stars flickered across my vision.

With a growl, I pushed away from the wall to face the men. Bob was bawling like a toddler as he tentatively touched his clearly broken nose. Unlike his buddy, Billy looked like a bull ready to charge out the gate as his furious gaze swung between his friend and me. That was one majorly pissed-off redneck that I now had to deal with.

He was too far away for me to reach with a kick or punch, but he was still blocking the hallway that led to the main area of the bar. I needed to get him to either give up and go away or come closer. Doubting there was anything at this point that would have him throwing in the towel, I weighed my options.

Running away would just have him

chasing me, and since he was so much taller, he'd catch me in no time. With him blocking the path to the main bar, I'd have to run out the rear exit, which wasn't a good plan at all. So, I really only had one option—fighting my way free. That meant I needed him to come closer. He was already so damn mad, I didn't think it would take much to push him over the edge to have him coming at me with all rage and no plan.

"Why don't you both just go walk this one off? You misjudged me as an easy target when I'm not. Keep this shit up and you'll both be going home knowing a little bit of a girl kicked your asses."

The way he squinted, clenching his hands into fists, had me thinking this plan was going the same way as all my others had for tonight, but it was way too late for second thoughts. Not that they'd left me with any other choice. Clenching my own fists and raising them up, ready to defend myself, I prayed I would make it out of this mess alive.

Chapter Two

Boone

Since I was about to get real damn busy with calving, I figured I'd make the most of having a night off to come down and enjoy some live music at The Barn while I could. I stood to the side of the pool tables with Jack, the owner of the honky tonk. We'd met in college and hit it off. Since my folks had to sell the family ranch and move into the city about a year before I'd completed my degree, when I did finish, I needed to pick somewhere to set up my own place. With nowhere else to go, I followed Jack out to southeastern Texas where he'd been born and raised, and settled in.

That had been twelve years ago and since then, we'd both grown our businesses to be successful. I'd bought a run-down ranch that had taken a lot of hard work to get back to being profitable, but I'd done it. Jack had taken over this honky tonk and classed it up a bit. Not so much that it had lost its roots, but enough he didn't have to have chicken wire surrounding the stage for the band's safety anymore, like it had been set-up when he'd first bought the place. These days it was doing good enough, he didn't need to be working his ass off behind the bar every night, which meant he could relax and have a few games of pool with me and some of our other friends on occasion.

Setting down my beer, I stepped up to the table for my shot when Jason, one of Jack's bartenders, came rushing up to him. The glint in his eyes had me turning my full attention to him.

"Jack, man, we got problems," Jason said. "You need to get down to the hallway near the ladies' bathroom, like, yesterday. Two redneck assholes have a woman jammed up down there."

Jack's expression turned dark enough to have the air feeling cooler. "Who reported it?"

"Had a young lady come to me just now to say she went back there to use the restroom but stopped short when she saw there were two men getting aggressive with a woman."

Jason was a great bartender, but he was a lover, not a fighter. It was not a shock he'd come to get his boss rather than trying to deal with the situation himself. Setting my stick on the table, I stepped up next to Jack.

"I'll come with you."

Liam, my full-time ranch hand who'd joined me tonight, stepped up too. "I'm in."

Jack looked me dead in the eye. "You sure? You ain't gonna lose your cool with this?"

Jack knew what had happened to my sister, and why men attacking a woman would be a huge trigger on my temper.

"No more than any other man. Let's get down there before they manage to get her outside."

With a nod, he turned to Jason. "Call the cops. Tell them to roll up to the rear entrance. No need to have the whole place up in this woman's business once we deal with her attackers."

He spun on his heal and strode off toward the bathrooms. Liam and I followed in his wake as Jason headed back to the bar to make the call. There were a few people hanging around the hallway entrance watching, and I wanted to knock each one of them into next week. None of these men or women were willing to step in to help the harassed woman, but were happy to watch her being attacked for entertainment? Some days society made me sick.

Jack pushed through the small crowd, telling them to get the hell out of there as he did. The bouncers who normally wandered hung around the door and stage area to keep things respectable came over and got the people moving. They were good guys and Jack could have tossed this to them and not worried about it, but he liked to be more hands-on than that.

We stepped into the dim hallway. One man was clutching his face and blood was dripping down from his nose. Looked like the woman was a fighter. *Good for her.*

"Why don't you both just go walk this one off? You misjudged me as an easy target but I'm not. Keep this shit up and you'll be going home knowing a little bit of a girl kicked your asses."

Her sweet voice drawled with a native Texan accent that did all sorts of inappropriate things to my body, considering the circumstances. I wanted to laugh at her words but taunting this bull of a man wasn't a wise move. Jack seemed to agree as he called out to distract the asshole before he could attack.

"What the fuck is going on down here?"

We kept moving toward them. The woman had shifted her stance and raised her fists like she was ready to take down her attacker.

Considering the state of the other guy, I didn't doubt she'd give it a red-hot go. But this redneck cowboy wannabe was big. He could do some damage to the little lady if he had a mind to. Her beauty caught my attention, holding it for a moment when I should have been focusing on the attackers.

Thankfully, Jack and Liam stepped in to end the stand-off. Jack grabbed the bigger man and threw him against the wall. One of Jack's hands was wrapped around the back of the asshole's neck, keeping him plastered to the sheetrock, while the other held his arm pinned up high behind his back, rendering the bastard fully immobile.

Liam had wrapped his hand around the injured man's bicep, letting him know he was being restrained but clearly not worried the man was any sort of real threat in his present state. If I wasn't mistaken, the man was actually blubbering over his busted-up face.

I moved closer to the silver-haired beauty, whose gaze flipped between each of us as though she was trying to decide if she was being saved or in more trouble than before. Even scared and roughed up, she was gorgeous.

"Ma'am? Are you okay?" I asked.

Gabs

Oh, wow. Now *this* man was a genuine cowboy. A black Stetson sat on his head, covering his hair, but the scruff along his jaw revealed he was a honey blond. His irises were the sweetest baby blue, and I could happily drown looking into them.

When a small sigh escaped me, it shocked me back into the moment. What the hell was I thinking?

"Let me go! She wanted what she was gettin'. Practically begged me for it!"

Billy's words had me seeing red and with a snarl, I spun to glare at him, trying to think of what I could do to hurt him while he was being restrained like he was. Turned out I didn't need to do a damn thing, as the man holding him shifted his grip from his neck to his hair and smacked his head against the wall to shut the idiot up.

"Ma'am?"

I turned my focus back to the gorgeous cowboy and gave him a small smile.

"I'm okay, thanks to y'all coming to my rescue in time. I really appreciate you stepping in."

I was sure someone in the bar had to have come down to use the bathrooms but instead of interfering or trying to help, they'd backed away and left me to it. People sucked sometimes.

His gaze ran over my face. When he got to my jaw, his every muscle seemed to tense, and an angry glint lit his eyes. When he started to raise a hand toward me, I jerked further down the hallway away from him. It didn't matter how pretty he was, I didn't know him and he could be worse than the two he'd helped save me from. He froze and then held up both palms in surrender.

"I won't hurt you, ma'am. My name's Boone and I'm trained in first aid. If it's okay, I'd like to take a look at that bruising on your face and the back of your head. I see you've got a little blood back there. I'd like to make sure we don't need to be calling an ambulance."

My eyes widened at the thought of ending up at hospital. As far as I knew, Bridgewater was the closest one, which meant basically the entire town would find out about me getting knocked around by morning. I didn't want to draw that level of attention to myself.

"Please, no ambulance. Honestly, I doubt any of the blood is mine." I nodded to Bob. "He grabbed me from behind and to get free, I head-butted him."

Boone's lips quirked up. "Good on you, honey."

"Broke my fuckin' nose!"

Bob's voice was a lot more nasally than it had been earlier. Boone's jaw tightened as he glared over at Bob but before he could speak, the cowboy holding Bob's arm tightened his grip until Bob's shoulder dropped from the pain.

"Be grateful that's all the lady broke."

Boone cleared his throat, and I looked back at him, getting caught in his baby blues again now that his expression had gentled once more.

I responded to his earlier request. "You can take a look."

He came in close, and I got my first lungful of his scent. Sage and leather... all man. I shivered when he touched his thumb and finger to my chin. His lips twitched, but he didn't say anything as he proceeded to gently prod at my cheek and jaw.

"Could you turn around, darlin'?"

"Sure."

I turned my back toward him and tried not to shiver again when his fingers ran up my neck and through my hair before he moved it around to look at my scalp. It didn't hurt too much when he prodded where I'd hit Bob, so I wasn't concerned about any real damage. I found myself missing the contact when he dropped his hands away from me.

"All done. You can turn back around if you'd like."

As I turned, the one holding Billy spoke up. "What's the verdict, Boone?"

Boone shifted his gaze from me to the other man.

"She'll be fine, Jack. Got a small lump on her head from where she took that one out, and her face is gonna be bruised up for a while, but nothing's broken." He returned his full attention to me. "Ma'am, do you feel lightheaded at all?"

He was back to the ma'ams. I much preferred how he drawled darlin'. Trying to stay focused on the situation at hand, not my inner, hopeless romantic's ramblings, I shook my head. "I highly doubt his head was hard enough to give me a concussion."

The cowboys scoffed out low chuckles before Jack said, "Boone, can you go grab some ice for her face? Ma'am, do you want to press charges?"

As much as I was calmer now that the incident was over, I was still mad as hell that those two had attacked me in the first place.

"Hell, yes, I want to press charges. Those two thought I was an easy mark and planned to drag me off and do who knows what to me. I'd hate to think what they would have managed to do if they'd grabbed a woman unable to fight back."

Billy tried to push Jack off him, forcing Jack to use his whole body to hold the bastard flush against the wall.

"There's nothin' to charge us for! She attacked us. You can see Bob's nose!" Billy managed to twist his head so he could glare at me, his gaze filled with fury. "Just you wait—"

Jack lifted away before slamming himself against Billy hard enough that it knocked the breath out of the bastard, thankfully cutting off his words.

"Just shut the fuck up already."

I moved to stand closer to Billy but made sure I kept Jack's body between us.

Despite the fact I knew the Charon MC would come to my aide at any time, and all I needed to do was ask, I tried to avoid going that route. The club tended to use more permanent solutions than I wanted on my conscience if I could help it. That, and I hated having to drag others into my messes. I preferred to clean up after myself. But more than any of that, was the fact I didn't want either of those assholes coming after me later on. If I worded things right, I might even be able to curb them from ever trying to pull this shit on any other woman again.

I caught Billy's gaze. "You ever heard of the Charon MC, Billy? Motorcycle club based down in Bridgewater?"

He stopped struggling against Jack's hold and frowned at me. "Yeah, who hasn't? What do they have to do with anything?"

The air in the hallway seemed to still around us as all the men waited for my answer.

"They've known me since I was a kid. Their vice president treats me as though I were his daughter. He's the *real* protective type, too. So, if you don't want me to press charges for the shit you pulled tonight, I could always give him a call instead. I'm sure he and a few of the guys would be more than happy to come up here and deal with you and Bob. Teach you the error of your ways and make sure neither of you ever attack another woman again. What do you say? Should I call him or have Jack call in the cops?"

The color had drained from his face and his eyes opened wide as I'd spoken. He didn't verbally respond, but I was satisfied he now understood how badly he'd fucked up picking me to attack tonight. I patted Jack on the shoulder before I returned to lean against the wall where I'd been.

"Call the cops, Jack. I doubt Billy-boy

really wants the other option of how we could clean this mess up."

Jack was focused on me. "Yeah, I don't really want to be on their bad side either. And the cops have already been called. They should be here any second."

I was nodding his way when the rear door banged open, and two deputies came striding toward us.

I was starting to wonder why I ever bothered to make plans, because they seemed to always end in disaster lately.

Chapter Three

Boone

I'D DONE my best to remain calm, not wanting to further upset or scare the woman, but now that I was facing away from her, I didn't bother to push down my fury. Seeing the nasty bruise over her cheek had brought back memories I tried my best to always keep locked away. This woman had been lucky. She'd been sober, and able to fight back against her attackers. Then we'd come in to help before it was too late.

Fourteen years ago, my sister, Summer, hadn't been so fortunate. Barely eighteen, she'd snuck into a New Year's Eve party with a few friends. Normally the quiet, good girl, Summer had been enjoying her little visit to the dark side—until she found herself separated from her friends and surrounded by a group of men who didn't care about the word "no".

I shook my head to empty those dark thoughts from my mind. I couldn't go back in time to fix things, but I could help this woman now. The cops would be here any moment, and she needed to get ice on her face. If I didn't get it to her before they pulled her aside to take her statement, she probably wouldn't bother icing it at all.

I pushed through to the bar and flagged down Jason.

"Everything okay back there?" he asked.

"Thanks to you, we got to her in time to prevent something more serious happening. She did take a hit to her face, though. Do you think you can put some ice in a towel for me?"

He gave me a nod and grinned. "I'll do you one better than that."

He vanished into the kitchen that was behind the bar and returned a few moments later with a commercial ice pack. He wrapped a couple of paper towels around it before he handed it over.

"There you go. Bring her up to the bar once she's done with the cops and we'll get her fed and a few drinks in her to make her feel better."

"Thanks, man."

I knew Jack wouldn't have an issue with Jason offering her whatever she wanted, on the house. They were both good men who'd never hesitate to take care of anyone, especially an innocent woman who'd been injured.

As I reached the head of the hallway, Jack was there with the woman beside him and a deputy following close behind.

"Thanks, Boone. Gonna let the deputy use my office to take her statement."

I handed her the ice pack. "Here you go, ma'am."

"Thank you."

She spoke softly but she had her chin held high. I was glad to see she wasn't going to let those bastards pull her down. I stalled out, getting lost looking at her. She really was beautiful, with that long, silver hair of hers and her big, brown eyes. She licked her lower lip and the sight of her tongue ring had me grinning. I'd thought I'd caught sight of a flash of metal in her mouth earlier but hadn't been sure. Made me wonder what else she was hiding under all her sweet cowgirl clothes. Although, considering the way she'd broken that fucker, Bob's, nose, it really shouldn't surprise me that she was more than she seemed on the surface. Clearly, the woman had a tough edge to her sweetness, which was basically my kryptonite. Nothing got to me more than a sweet woman who had no issue with getting her hands a little dirty when needed. I could easily see her out on my ranch.

"My office is this way."

Jack's words shook me free from my trance, and I stepped out of the way.

Liam stayed back with me as the others moved away. "C'mon, let's go grab a beer."

I trailed after Liam, keeping an eye on the trio as they headed into Jack's office until the door closing blocked my view. Thankfully, Liam picked a spot close by and as I slipped onto a stool beside him, Jason was quick to set a fresh beer in front of both of us.

"There you go, boys."

I gave him a nod. "Thanks."

The first mouthful was ice cold and did wonders for making me feel better as it went down.

"She's an interesting lady, that's for sure."

I stiffened at Liam's words. Was he interested in her too? I didn't want to compete with him for her attention. I didn't hit on women my friends were interested in. It wasn't who I was, but dammit, I wanted at least a chance with this one.

"Calm down, Boone. I ain't sniffing at her skirts. Anyone with half a brain can see you fancy her. I just figured you'd appreciate a heads up on what came out while you were fetching that ice pack."

Setting the bottle on the bar, I turned to face him. "I was gone for less than ten minutes. What the hell could have happened that quickly?"

"Oh, buddy. So much." He smirked at me and took a drink from his beer while I contemplated knocking him off his stool.

"Liam, quit teasing the man before he hits you." Jack came and stood between us, signaling Jason for his own drink. With every passing second, my curiosity was heading toward pissed off.

"Do you think one of you could tell me what the fuck happened before she gets done with the deputy?"

Jack rested a palm on my shoulder. "Your girl has ties to the Charon MC, my friend. Good luck with that."

I shrugged off his hand and turned to face him. "She ain't my girl. Hell, I don't even know her name! And that lady ain't no biker chick. No way."

"Yeah, I wouldn't have guessed it either, but she said so herself. Told Billy if he didn't want the police involved, she could always call the club in. Apparently, their VP thinks of her as a daughter. Her name is Gabriela

Rayne, and we all saw how you were eyeballing her."

I picked up my beer for another drink as I rolled that information around, ignoring the ribbing my two friends were giving me. Gabriela was a beautiful name. I wondered what she did for work, where she lived. The Charon MC was based down in Bridgewater, about half an hour from here. Was that where she lived?

Jack nudged my shoulder. "They're done. You gonna go grab your girl or do you want me to?"

I slipped off the stool to his and Liam's laughter.

"Fuck off, both of you."

I headed toward the silver-haired beauty who was looking a little lost as she watched the deputy walk away from her.

"Ma'am? Care to join me at the bar for a drink or two, some food? Jack told Jason you can have anything you want on the house tonight. Be a shame to waste an offer like that now, wouldn't it?"

Gabs

Was the hot cowboy flirting with me? Or had Jack told him to keep me safe and happy so I wouldn't have any reason to call in the Charons?

After what had just happened, I really shouldn't even care if this cowboy was interested, because I shouldn't be interested in him. But I was. For some reason, Boone held my attention like no other man ever had. I wasn't ready to go home. Billy and Bob were gone, and the ice had helped get rid of the swelling and redness on my face, so there was nothing stopping me from still enjoying my night here at The Barn.

"Well, I guess we'd better take advantage of the hospitality then. I mean, it'd be rude not to, right?"

As I moved toward the bar, he slid his hand around me, resting it against my lower back. The touch was barely there, but I felt it all the way to my toes. A shiver ran through me, and I prayed he didn't notice.

The other two men who'd come to my rescue along with Boone—Jack, who I'd learned was the owner of The Barn, and Liam, another cowboy—were both at the bar, smirking over at us. I wasn't entirely sure what they found so funny, but I really couldn't be bothered to try to figure it out. I was too busy enjoying the feel of Boone's hand against my back.

I'd been called a hopeless romantic and a dreamer more than a few times during my life. I couldn't help it. Despite my history of finding the wrong men, I was still hopeful that somewhere out there, my Prince Charming was waiting for me. If he happened to come wearing a cowboy hat and oozed southern charm, all the better.

As we got to the bar, Jack shifted the empty seat next to him out a little so I could slip onto it.

"Gabriela, let me apologize again for what happened to you earlier."

I held my palm up to stop him. "It's not your fault in any way, Jack. I certainly don't hold you responsible for what those two bastards tried to pull tonight. I'm grateful you run such a tight ship that you were notified about it so quickly and could come to my rescue."

Jack chuckled. "In your defense, ma'am, you seemed to have it under control when we stepped in."

Heat flared in my cheeks. Sure, I'd taken care of Bob, but if they hadn't shown up when they had, Billy could have really hurt me. I was sure they all knew that. A change of subject was needed.

"Boone tells me you're covering my bill for the night?"

He grinned. "That's right." He nodded toward the bartender who was coming toward us. "Just tell Jason what you want, and he'll get it for you, on the house."

Jason was a good-looking man, in a very metrosexual way. He had long, blond hair up in a man bun with a neatly trimmed beard. His eyes looked kind, and they filled with sympathy as he got to us.

"Hey, there, darlin'. You doing okay? Need another ice pack?"

I pressed my fingers against the side of my face as his gaze ran over it.

"The swelling has mostly gone down now, so I think I'm good. But I'll let you know if I change my mind." I winced. "Sorry, I left the first one back in Jack's office. Do you want me to go grab it?"

He shook his head. "No need. Plenty more in the freezer and someone will take care of that other one later. How about something to eat?"

"I could definitely go for some food. What's good here?"

As Jason began to rattle off the menu, he poured a soda and set the glass in front of me before turning away to grab a shot glass and fill it with more of the whiskey I had earlier. I grinned at him when he set it down next to the soda.

"You remembered what I ordered earlier?"

He gave me a wink. "Darlin', it's my job to remember. So, what can I get you from the kitchen?"

"That loaded mac and cheese sounded delicious."

"The best kind of comfort food there is. I'll put the order in for you and bring it over when it's done. You staying here at the bar or sitting at a table?"

A glance around showed that people were watching me, and I couldn't help but hear them whispering about what had gone down earlier. I wanted to be anywhere but at the bar where everyone could see me. Boone's large hand returned to my lower back, and he moved in close enough I caught another lungful of his sage and leather scent.

"We'll go sit over by the pool tables, Jason."

Jason set down three more beers before he headed back toward the kitchen to place my order.

"C'mon, Gabriela," Boon said, "it's quieter back there. Not so many people watching."

His warm palm moved around my side and over my hip before he guided me gently to the edge of the stool. As I slipped off, I stumbled and pressed a palm against his torso to steady myself. My breath caught at the hard, warm muscles that greeted my fingers. My mind filled with what he might look like under the shirt.

Liam's low chuckle had me shaking my head and dropping my hand away.

Turning toward the bar, I downed the whiskey before taking my soda and turning back toward Boone. He had an eyebrow raised at me.

"What? Never seen a woman shoot whiskey before?"

"Well, not often."

I gave him a wink and stepped away from the bar toward the pool tables. Within a few steps, his palm returned to my back, guiding me until we reached an empty table against the rear wall behind the pool tables. After setting my glass down, I sat on one of the seats, hating that it meant I lost Boone's hand against my back. He took the seat beside me while Liam sat opposite us.

"Jack'll be over later, I'm sure."

I shrugged at Liam's words. "I'm sure he's a busy man. Way too busy to be able to babysit me the rest of the night." I moved my gaze between the two men. "Just like you both probably have other things…"

My words dried up when Boone shifted in his seat, so his whole body faced me not the table.

"Gabriela, we're not spending time with you because Jack told us to. We're here because we want to be. Try to relax, forget about those two morons, and enjoy your night. Once you eat, we'll play a few games of pool, maybe dance some."

I got a little lost in his baby blues as he spoke, and had no clue what to say to him.

Liam's voice cut through the moment. "I'm mainly here to watch Boone make a fool of himself, but yeah, no one's making me stay either, sugar."

There was humor laced in his words, but he had that wrong. I was the one making a fool of myself.

"Here you go. Loaded mac and cheese for the lady, and some nachos for the men so they don't steal your mac and cheese."

Jack placed the plates down on the table before moving to sit at the empty seat and joining us. The aroma was divine and before my stomach could start growling, I lifted the fork to eat while half listening to the men talk about how calving season was about to start and how busy they'd be once it did, except for

Jack, who'd be quieter because so many of his regulars were ranchers. Instead of joining their conversation as I ate, I busied myself imagining Boone on the back of a horse, rounding up cattle and helping mama cows birth their calves. Did he even have horses? I knew some ranchers preferred four wheelers to horses and I needed to know if he was one of them.

"Do you have horses?"

Boone turned his full attention to me again, and those baby blues of his lit up with interest, which had me sitting a little straighter as a wave of hope rolled through me while I waited for his answer.

Boone

Gabriela asking about horses was a guaranteed way to get her my full attention. She wouldn't have asked if she didn't like the animals, would she? With each new thing I learned about her, aside from the biker stuff, she was drawing me in more and more.

"You like horses, Gabriela?"

Her grin widened. "Please, call me Gabs. Everyone does. And, yeah, I *love* horses."

"Oh, this is too good," Liam murmured.

Praying Gabs hadn't heard him, I pretended like I hadn't either.

"I own the Phoenix Star Ranch down near Bridgewater. I have three horses at the moment. A stallion and two mares."

Moving her plate aside, she rested her elbow on the table and propped up her chin on her hand. "You said 'at the moment.' Does that mean you normally have more?"

I shook my head. "I want to be able to take more in. Aside from the cattle ranch, I volunteer with the SPCA as a cruelty investigator. My dream is to have a horse rescue, but that costs money so the cattle are a necessity. It's a balancing act with time and money as to how many rescues I can take in."

She sat straighter, dropping her arm off the table.

"Do you have other animals you've rescued, or just the horses?"

She was too good to be true. Not only did she like horses, but she was interested in animal rescue too. Liam and Jack were sitting back, lifting their beers up to hide their smirks. They both knew me well enough to know this woman had my number.

"I've been known to take in all sorts of animals until we can find them a long-term home. I think the pair of goats were the most memorable. Damn, those critters eat everything."

She laughed. "Yeah, but they're cute."

That had me smirking. "The horns aren't cute when they use them on you, head butting you until you'll drop whatever you happen to be holding so they can eat it. Nor are the holes in the sheets after they took a liking to them when I'd hung them out on the line."

She tried to contain her laughter, but a chuckle snuck out. Clearly, she found the destruction of my life by those goats hilarious. Looking back at it, I could see the funny side myself. But at the time, not so much.

"Do you work with animals at all?" I asked.

She smirked as her eyes sparkled. "Well, that depends on your definition of what's an animal. I'm a piercer and tattooist at Silky Ink down in Bridgewater. Some of my clientele could probably be described as animals."

She gave me a sweet wink as she reached for her soda to take a drink.

I shook my head. "You're just full of surprises, darlin'."

She lowered her drink but didn't put it down. "What do you mean?"

"You dress all sweet cowgirl, but you take down men with head butts, have a tongue piercing, and now I find out you pierce and tattoo people for a living. Not at all what I was expecting."

She tilted the glass my way. "Don't forget the whole biker thing."

She was fishing to see if the others had told me what she'd said in the hallway after I left.

"Yeah, that too."

She grinned and took another drink, finishing it off before she set it down on the table.

"Meanwhile, cowboy, you are just as you look. A hard-working rancher who loves animals."

I coughed as heat flared over my cheeks. Damn woman was making me blush.

I shrugged. "Don't see the point in trying to be someone I'm not."

She stiffened a little and I winced at how she could have taken my words as an insult.

"I'm not—"

She stopped me with a wave of her hand.

"I know what you meant. And to be honest, I'm not hiding my real self either. I love animals and ranch life. I'm also creative. Silk, the woman who owns Silky Ink, has been my best friend since we were twelve. We decided in school we'd set up the shop, and that's what we went on to do. I love my work, but it's not my only passion. I rent a trailer on the corner of a property and help out with my landlord's horses when I can."

Her expression turned sad, and a sheen of tears glossed over her eyes before she turned to stare down into her empty glass. "Well, I used to help with their horses. So yeah, wearing cowboy boots and jeans is showing the real me, just like wearing a dress and heels in the shop is."

I leaned forward and hooking a finger under her chin, tilted her face back to me. She had teared up but was fighting them back.

"Why can't you help out with the horses anymore? What happened?"

"I rent my trailer from the older couple who own the ranch with the horses. Their son has recently returned home, and, well, long story short, he pulled some shit tonight and now I'm banned from the barn."

I ran my gaze over her face, noting the sadness in her brown eyes. She was gutted at the ban.

"I'm real sorry, darlin'. Is that why you came here tonight?"

She nodded slightly, not saying a word as though she didn't trust her voice.

"Well, I'm about to get real busy with calving, but I'm sure I can make some time for you to come over and meet my horses, if you want. Triton, my stallion, can be a bit high strung, but Stormy and Bolt will love you the moment you give them a few apple slices."

Her eyes lit up, and I knew I'd said the right thing. I was going to be busy as hell and dog tired for the next few months, but I would push all that aside to make time for this woman.

"Are you serious?"

"Wouldn't offer if I didn't mean it, Gabs. Give me your phone and I'll put my number in. Let me know the next time you have a few hours free, and I'll see if I can make it work."

She pulled from my touch, slipped her phone from her pocket, unlocked the screen then handed it over. I quickly tapped in my number, saved it, then sent a text to my phone so I had hers. When I handed the phone back, the grin she gave me was like a rising sun.

I'd be willing to do just about anything to see it again.

When a slower song started, I gave her a smile. "How about we take a turn on the dance floor? I'll do my best to not trample your toes."

Still smiling, she rose to stand and when I reached for her hand, she slid hers into mine. I ignored Jack and Liam, who were both doing a really bad job of trying to hide their snickering at me. They could do and say whatever the hell they wanted. I was the lucky one heading to the dance floor with the silver-haired beauty holding my hand.

Monday 22 January 2018

Gabs

Sunday passed in a blur and when Monday rolled around, I was still floating on cloud nine, thinking about Boone. Even with that distraction, my anger at Royce preventing me from spending time with the horses—especially Whiskey—still burned bright. The beautiful liver chestnut mare had bonded with me just as I had with her over the last two years.

I'd been trying to think of a way around Royce's dictate, sure his father didn't know about what he'd done. I needed to get John alone, but I hadn't seen him at all over the weekend. Which had me worried for more than one reason. If he and Kate were seriously ill, I wasn't sure Royce would call in medical help for them. I had wondered if calling them would connect ush, but I didn't want to risk Royce answering the phone.

I didn't want to get evicted from my

home, which I feared Royce was spiteful enough to do. Maybe I could sneak over to the barn in the early morning. It was a huge risk and if Royce did catch me, I knew he'd definitely kick me out of my trailer.

I tapped my fingers on the steering wheel as I drove to work, thinking over the issue.

Not being able to spend time with Whiskey and the other horses was an ache in my soul. Thankfully, I had memories of Boone from Saturday night to keep me sane. Like the way he'd laid the sweetest goodnight kiss on my lips when we'd finally left The Barn in the wee hours of the morning.

I'd wanted to call him so many times yesterday but resisted the urge, not wanting to ruin things by coming across as being desperate. Even if I was feeling that way about my sexy cowboy.

When I arrived at Silky Ink, I was still lost in my daydreaming. I hummed as I headed straight to the counter to check the appointment book to see what my week looked like, hoping I had an evening or two clear, so I could meet up with Boone. Calving season was an insanely busy time on a ranch and dragged on for months, but I didn't want to have to wait till it was all over to see him again. Even if it meant I'd have to help him with work.

"What happened over the weekend that has that look on your face?"

I glanced over at Silk, who'd just come through from the rear of the shop. She reached the counter and stood beside me, looking over my shoulder at the appointment book. She was already mentally moving on from her question even though I hadn't answered her yet.

I blinked back the sudden sting of tears as I shrugged. "Just in a good mood this morning."

There was a time, not long ago, that I would have told Silk all about Boone. Hell, before she'd met Eagle and settled into marital bliss, she'd have been my first phone call once I'd gotten home, no matter how late it was. Well, considering we'd lived together back then, I wouldn't have needed to actually call her. If she hadn't been with me when I went out, I would have gone straight to her room and told her all about how awesome Boone was.

But that felt like a lifetime ago now. Silk was married and had a son. Raven was the cutest little thing. Five months old, he was all sweet smiles and big eyes. At least, to the outside world that's how he looked. I could tell just looking at Silk, she wasn't getting enough sleep. Raven was teething and not happy about it.

I didn't begrudge my friend her life. Not at all. But I was a little envious. She had everything I'd always craved, always planned to have. Things she'd often said she didn't need in her life. It didn't seem fair that fate had handed it all to her while skipping over me. But that wasn't Silk's fault. I was happy for her, truly. I just missed my best friend. Missed having someone I could talk to about anything. I was also sad that we weren't going through this stage of our lives together. We were supposed to settle down and have families at the same time.

My thoughts went back to Boone. He'd been wonderful Saturday night, asking about my life, looking worried when I'd told him about not being able to see Whiskey anymore. Could he be who I needed? Would he think I was too much or clingy if I started telling him everything? Or would he see me in the same light, letting me be his go-to person too?

He volunteered with the SPCA. That had to mean he saw all sorts of horrible cases of animal abuse. Who did he go to when he needed to decompress from that? Was that what The Barn was for him?

Shaking all those thoughts from my mind, I looked back to the schedule. I had a fairly full week, but I might be able to rearrange things on Wednesday to be able to give myself an early night. I pulled my phone out and before I could talk myself out of it, sent a text off to Boone, letting him know when I was going to be available this week.

Donny and SeVen came through from the back, chatting to each other at the same time the first clients for the day came in the front door. My phone buzzing in my pocket made me smile. I couldn't look at it yet but knowing Boone responded so quickly had me smiling.

As I led my first client back to the piercing room, I sent up a little prayer that things would work out with the handsome cowboy, even if every other part of my life was a mess at the moment.

Chapter Four

Tuesday 20ᵗʰ February 2018

Boone

It had been a month since that night at The Barn when I'd met Gabs, and we'd both been so busy in that time we hadn't managed more than several phone calls and a whole lot of texts. Every calving season was the same. It was a predictably busy time of year for all ranchers, but I'd been hopeful I'd be able to fit in seeing my beauty. I hadn't anticipated her work schedule being so full. I hadn't thought a tattooist and piercer would be as busy as she was. Apparently, their shop had a good reputation and drew clients in from outside the area. I guessed it also helped to be so closely tied to a motorcycle club. Whenever I'd seen bikers wearing a club vest, they always seemed to be covered in ink.

After so much time passing since seeing her and only getting one goodnight kiss from her that first time, I couldn't wait to see her again and finally, today was that day. She had the afternoon and evening off work, so she was coming over to spend the time with me on the ranch. I'd still need to get a few chores done while she was here, but I figured she could join me for them.

Since she loved horses so much, I planned on leaving the ATV home and saddling up a couple of the horses to go check the herd. I had a picnic dinner all packed and ready to go, so once we finished, we could go for a ride. Being spring, it was pretty damn muddy at the moment, but one of the pastures had an area of rocks. A few of them were large and flat enough that we'd be able to spread out our picnic on them. I knew, because my three nieces loved to have picnics out there whenever they came over.

Anticipation at finally getting some alone time with Gabs had me rushing through the day. By the time I stood on the front porch watching her car come up the driveway, I was strung as tight as a new fence. I didn't move while she pulled up then got out, taking a few moments to soak in the sight of her. She wore jeans, boots, and a long sleeve button down shirt. With a straw hat on her head, she was all cowgirl, and I couldn't help but grin at the picture she made.

When she started walking toward me, I made my way down the stairs and when I reached her, wrapped an arm around her waist and pulled her in flush against me. Before she could say a word, I curled a finger under her chin, tilting her face up so I could take her mouth with mine. The moment our lips touched, I was lost to her. The feel of her against me, her scent in my lungs, overtook my mind until I could think about was her, just like the first time.

She slipped her palms up my front and rested them on my pecs, her touch burning through my shirt as she leaned into me. With a moan, I tightened my hold on her and deepened the kiss, swiping my tongue over her lower lip until she opened for me to slip inside. Her sweet taste exploded through me and drove my need for this woman higher. With a groan, I pulled back from the contact before we got so carried away, I completely forgot about all we had to get done.

"Damn, sweetheart. I wish we could take this inside and keep going—"

She cut me off by pressing a quick kiss to my lips.

"I get it, Bo. We've got jobs to do first, but I'm all yours till morning, so we'll have plenty of time later. You know, if that's what you want."

Her cheeks flushed.

"Gabs, I'd like nothing better than to have you stay over. Been missing you like crazy."

Which was nuts considering we barely knew each other, but it was the God's honest truth.

"Me, too. C'mon, let's go get these chores done. We going out on the ATV or the horses?"

Forcing myself to release her from my embrace, I took her hand and led her to the barn.

"I figured we'd take the horses for a ride, then once we're done checking on the herd, we can ride up to a perfect little spot I know for some supper."

She gave my hand a squeeze and grinned up at me when I glanced over to her. She was completely adorable, and the fact she appeared to love ranch life? Well, that was the cherry on the top. She seemed so damn perfect, I was on edge waiting for the dream to end. I hadn't had a whole lot of perfect or easy in my life. And this thing with Gabs was going so smoothly, I was struggling to trust it was for real.

Gabs

I couldn't stop smiling as I led Stormy, one of Boone's rescued mares, out of the barn. She was a dapple grey, so looked nothing like Whiskey, who I missed terribly. It'd been a month since Royce had told me I was no longer welcome in their barn. I'd tried to keep myself as busy as I could, so I didn't think too much about the horses I'd grown to love so much. The other reason I kept busy was to avoid being home alone. I'd found trampled plants around my windows more than once since Royce had pulled his shit, and I was starting to accept the fact I was going to have to move soon.

The downside to being so busy was how difficult it had been to line up some free time with Boone. I'd not taken that fact into consideration when I opened up my schedule at Silky Ink. Bookings had flooded in before I realized my mistake.

The idea of spending the rest of the day not only with Boone, but riding and being around horses was enough to put a bounce in my step.

When I'd gone past the other rescued mare, Bolt, she'd looked so damn sad as she watched me saddle up Stormy then leave her behind. Telling her I'd take her next time didn't seem to help her mood.

I glanced over to speak to Boone, but the sight of him mounting his large, black stallion, Triton, had me freezing. Damn, he filled out his Wranglers well, and the sight of him in that saddle made my mouth go dry.

Once he got settled atop his horse, he looked in my direction with a smirk. "Like what you see, darlin'?"

Heat raced over my cheeks as I turned my focus to mounting Stormy, ignoring his question as I settled myself into the saddle.

"Do you think I could take out Bolt for a quick ride after we get back?"

He chuckled as he caught my gaze. He knew I was changing the subject to avoid answering his question. "You caught her giving us the stink eye as we went past her too, huh? We'll give her some lovin' when we get back, make it up to her."

I walked Stormy over toward him, and once I got near, Boone tugged the reins, urging Triton forward. I followed his lead as we headed away from the barn.

South Texas was mostly flat, so I could see for quite a way in each direction. My heart swelled as I stilled to inhale a deep breath of the country air and take it all in.

"You doin' all right?"

"Yeah, just taking a moment to appreciate all this."

Boone turned to scan the view as though he hadn't seen it before. Guess he mostly kept his head down while he worked. Which was a damn shame. He had beautiful property.

"So, what are we going to do, exactly?" I spoke as we led the horses through the gate and Boone latched it before he answered.

"Twice a day, I come out and check the cows to make sure none are in distress with birthing. It shouldn't take much time, as long as everything is fine."

I followed his lead and mounted then we moved around the pasture to check on the various groups of cattle. Many calves had already been born and they were the cutest things ever. Part of me wanted to hop down and pet each and every one. Boone chuckled and my cheeks heated once more.

"What?"

"You are so damn adorable, sugar. All your sweet little noises as we find each new calf."

I shrugged a shoulder. "Not like I get to see baby animals too often, and even you have to admit they are so stinkin' cute. Just look at them! Big, brown eyes—oh, and that one has a heart-shaped splotch between its eyes. *Naw.*"

With a shake of his head and a big grin, he moved further around the herd, and I followed him.

"Oh, shit. Well, that'll teach me for saying this won't take long."

I sat straighter in the saddle and followed his gaze. A lone cow stood next to a group of trees. Her head was down, and she looked miserable.

"What's wrong with her?"

I figured it was something to do with a calf, but I wasn't sure what.

He slowly led us over toward the animal before dismounting and moving to one of the bags he had attached to his saddle.

"She's been in labor for a while by the looks of things. She's tired but for some reason, the calf ain't coming on its own." He turned to look me straight in the eye. "She's too worn out to bring her back to the pens. Are you all right to help me? If you're not, that's fine. I'll manage. It'll just be a lot easier with your help."

I licked my suddenly dry lips before I could answer him.

"Of course, I'll help. But I've never done anything like this before. I have no clue what to do."

I dismounted and he came over, took my chin between his thumb and finger, then tilted my face so he could give me a quick kiss that left me melting a little more for this man.

"You're the best, sugar." He released his hold and stood straighter. "Just drop Stormy's reins to the ground. She's been trained to stay ground tied."

With a deep breath and a roll of his sexy, broad shoulders, he turned back toward the cow. "First up, I need to catch her, then I'll get you to hold her steady while I help her get this calf out."

I ran my gaze over the large animal. "Um, Bo? She's kind of big. Like a lot bigger than me. How am I gonna be able to keep her steady?"

He glanced back to me with a smile. "You'll be fine, sugar. I'd never let you get hurt. Once I catch her, I'll bend one of her forelegs at the knee. That'll hobble her. As long as you hold that foreleg bent, she won't move. And, Gabs, this girl is tired and looking for some help. She shouldn't give us too much trouble."

I gave him a nod and he flew into action, rushing toward the cow and getting a hold of her neck before gripping the foreleg and bending it up, just as he'd said he would. She mooed at him but didn't thrash. Circling around the animal, I moved to stand beside Boone, and he grabbed my wrist to guide my hand to take the place of his.

"Here, just hold this leg up like this."

Doing as instructed, I watched as he retrieved chains from the bag. Wondering what exactly he was planning to do, I frowned as he disappeared from my view behind the animal with them. I thought he'd just reach in with his hand and pull out the calf, not use thick, metal chains. Since I didn't want to distract him, I figured I'd ask about the mechanics of what he was doing later.

As the sun moved closer to the horizon, I tried to block out the noises coming from behind the cow and instead focused on her, making soothing sounds to the animal. She seemed content to stay put, not trying to get her leg free so I could hold her with one hand and use the other to stroke her head.

This wasn't how I'd thought the night would go, but I wasn't complaining. I was glad to be able to help Boone. I wasn't sure how he'd do this on his own. And hopefully, this wouldn't take too long then we could get back to our previous plans.

We had all night to spend together, after all.

Chapter Five

Boone

GABS WAS A TROOPER. She stayed holding the mama cow the entire time it took me to turn the calf around, put the chains on the front hooves, then get Triton to help me pull it free. She didn't try to look around the cow and had her head close to the animal's, murmuring to it. That made me smile.

When it was all over, Gabs released her hold on the cow's foreleg and came over to me. I wanted to sling my arm around her shoulders and pull her in close against me, but I was covered in bloody mess so resisted the urge as we both stood side by side and watched the calf as it took its first steps, with its mama giving it a once over before beginning to lick it clean.

"You did great, darlin'."

She scoffed at me. "I didn't do much. You're the one who did all the work. Why the chains?"

I decided not to get too detailed with the description. Gabs had been a star doing everything I asked of her, but the fact she clearly hadn't wanted to see the action had me thinking she wouldn't appreciate a blow-by-blow account of it, either.

"They're special OB chains. I wrapped one around each of the forelegs, then with Triton's help, pulled the calf out."

She nodded and moved to press against me, but I stepped away. "Whoa. As much as I'd love to cuddle, I'm covered in muck you probably don't want to share, darlin'."

"Eww. Yeah, guessing this has put a cramp in our dinner plans."

I had to laugh at the expression on her face as she took in my body. I preferred the heated look she gave me earlier to this disgusted one, but she still looked as adorable as all get-out.

"C'mon, let's ride back and get the horses put up, then I'll clean up and we can eat back at the house. We can do the picnic another day."

She nodded. "I'll spend some time with Bolt while you clean up. She looked so damn miserable when we rode out earlier."

I bit the inside of my cheek to stop myself from laughing as I mounted Triton.

"You're gonna spoil all my animals. First you pet and coddle my cattle. Now, you're gonna have my horses expecting all sorts of benefits."

"Daisy earned it. And look at how cute her little baby is."

I shook my head as I got sorted to get moving. I'd been wondering if she'd named the cow. Now I had my answer.

"So, you planning on naming the entire herd?"

She grinned as she guided Stormy to walk beside Triton and me. "Figure I'll just call all the girls Daisy. You have way too many to go naming them all individually." She cleared her throat and shrugged a shoulder. "I had to call her something while I was petting and talking to her."

Then she leaned forward to stroke her palm down Stormy's neck. "And I'll spoil your horses as much as you'll let me. I miss Whiskey and the other horses I used to see nearly every day."

My heart broke a little for her. Her landlord's son was an asshole to cut her off like that. No way could I give up all my animals on a dime like she'd been forced to do. Sure, the horses hadn't technically been hers, but she'd explained how she helped take care of them over the past year or so. She'd bonded with them, and now she wasn't allowed to see them. I knew how much that hurt.

While I'd been away at college, my parents had sold the family ranch and all the animals, including the horses I'd grown up taking care of. It had been a serious blow to my soul, but I understood why they'd done it. The attack on my sister had left her pregnant with triplets. Both during the pregnancy and while the girls had been babies, she'd needed to be close to medical care, but she'd also needed our folks to be there for her, too.

Unlike my grandfather and me, my dad didn't get the ranching gene. He did it because it was what he knew, not because it was something that was in his blood, and he couldn't live without. He'd been happy to sell up and move closer to town to help Summer with the girls. Also meant he could follow his real passion, carpentry.

I leaned forward so I could stroke Triton's neck.

"You're welcome out here whenever you want, Gabs. The horses would love to have you out here lovin' on them whenever you can manage it."

"Just the horses?" Her voice went low, with a sexy rasp to it.

I turned toward her with a smirk. "Darlin', you know damn well that I'm always happy to see you."

She gave me a wink and a grin that had my body coming alive and left me trying to discreetly rearrange myself in the saddle because riding with a hard-on wasn't much fun. I sure as hell didn't want to slow our ride down. It wouldn't be long before I had my silver-haired beauty all to myself in the privacy of my home.

I couldn't wait.

Gabs

I'd just pulled the saddle off Stormy when my phone started ringing. I ignored the first call as I had my hands full, but when it rang a second time after I'd put the saddle away, I pulled it out of my pocket. Seeing it was my brother, I answered it straight away.

"Hello? Christopher? What's up?"

He rarely called, so I was on alert.

"Hey, Gabs. Ah, are you sitting down?"

I frowned. What the hell was going on?

"Why do I need to be sitting down,

Christopher? Just tell me what's going on already."

"Mom and Dad were in a wreck earlier."

I stopped moving as all my blood rushed south, leaving me dizzy.

"What? Are they okay? When did it—"

"Whoa, slow down with the questions, sis. They were heading out of Houston, back toward Bridgewater, when a truck's brakes failed and took them, along with three other cars, out at a set of lights."

Tears sprang forth and I didn't bother trying to stop them.

My voice cracked as I asked my next question. "Are they okay?"

"They're both in surgery at the moment."

My brother was a plastic surgeon, for fuck's sake. I knew he would have more information than that.

"Tell me, Christopher! I know you wouldn't be happy with just knowing they were in surgery."

He sighed into the phone. "Mom's right shoulder and arm are a mess, she's also got some internal bleeding. I honestly don't know exactly what her injuries are at this stage, and I won't until she gets out of surgery. Dad was driving. They had to cut him out of the vehicle. His left leg was crushed. The doctor wasn't sure if he'd be able to save the limb."

I covered my mouth as a sob tore free while I tried to process what my brother was telling me. It was too much. My parents weren't that old, only in their late fifties. Surely, they were young enough to be able to recover from their injuries. Even if my father lost his leg, he'd still be here with us. Right?

My brother continued, cutting off my spiraling thoughts, "So, yeah, it's going to be a long recovery for them both, but it looks like they'll both pull through. Some of the other victims weren't so lucky, Gabs. It was a mess."

Even though he couldn't see me, I nodded, too choked up to speak. *Lucky to be alive…* a phrase I never thought I'd hear in regard to my parents.

"What hospital?"

"Memorial Herman, here in Houston."

The hospital where he worked. "I'm on my way."

"Gabs, seriously, take your time. There's no rush. They're both going to be in surgery for a while yet. The last thing I need is for you to crash too because you're upset and driving. Maybe get Silk to come with you?"

It warmed me a little that Christopher cared. There were times I honestly wondered about how he felt about me.

"I'll be careful. And, yeah, I'll work something out."

I wouldn't bother Silk with this. She was too busy with her new family.

"Okay, well, let me know when you leave so I know when to expect you in. Love you, sis."

"Love you too, bro. See you soon."

Ending the call, I stalled out and stood there staring at the dark screen. I was numb as I tried to process how my world had just been turned on its head with one phone call.

Boone's large palm slipped up my spine and wrapped around the back of my neck. The warmth of his skin against mine helped ground me. I turned and looked up into his beautiful, baby blue irises.

"My parents were in a crash."

He nodded once. "Want me to come with you? You shouldn't be alone, Gabs."

I glanced around to see that he'd been busy while I was on the phone. The horses were back in their stalls, and everything appeared to be done.

"Um, if you don't mind?"

I couldn't admit out loud how scared I was, how much I didn't want to drive into Houston alone.

"You need me, I'm there, Gabs. Just give me ten minutes to get cleaned up and changed, then we'll head off. Okay?"

He took off my hat and pressed a kiss to

my temple that melted my insides before returning my hat to my head.

"C'mon, beautiful, let's go inside. You can grab yourself something to eat while I clean up."

Chapter Six

Gabs

With a firm grip on Boone's hand, I walked through the hospital front doors. I'd messaged Christopher as Boone parked and he'd responded that he'd meet us in the lobby to take us back to the family waiting room, so I wasn't surprised to find him standing off to the side with his hands in his pockets.

He stood straighter before coming toward us. I dropped Boone's hand and rushed to hug my brother. He awkwardly wrapped an arm around me and patted my back. He hadn't ever been great with accepting affection, but he'd always tried with me.

"Hey, Gabs, Mom's in recovery, but not awake yet. I'm still waiting on word about

Dad. Who's this? I didn't know you were seeing anyone."

I pulled back and closing my eyes, took a deep breath at the relief that Mom at least was out of surgery. Opening my eyes, I turned to smile at Boone, who came up and wrapped an arm around my waist, pulling me in against his strength.

"Christopher, this is Boone. Boone, my brother, Christopher."

Boone reached out a hand to shake my brother's. "Hey, nice to meet you, although I would have preferred it to be under better circumstances."

Christopher gave him a nod before he turned his attention back to me. "Follow me and we'll go back to the family waiting room. Not sure how long it'll take before we hear anything on Dad, but we should be able to visit Mom soon."

Slipping my hand back into Boone's, I followed Christopher through the hospital until we came to a small waiting room. It was much smaller than the main one and more private. Clearly for people waiting on news, there was no one coughing or sick in here, which I appreciated. The few other people in the space were to one side, so Christopher led us to the opposite side.

"When's Silk getting here?"

I frowned over at Christopher as I sat in one of the hard, plastic chairs. "Huh? Why would Silk be coming in?"

He rolled his eyes. "Gabs, you two have done everything together for over a decade. Kinda expected she would have been your first call after I rang you earlier. What's going on? Did you two have a fight or something?"

I shrugged, not liking how both men were looking at me expectantly, like I was about to reveal some big secret.

"She's married with a baby now. Nothing's happened, she's just busy these days, that's all. We're not kids anymore, Christopher. We don't live in each other's pockets."

I looked down at my hands as I picked at my nails. The truth was, I missed Silk and the closeness we used to have. And as much as I loved that Boone had come with me and Christopher was here too, having Silk would have been nice. But I wasn't going to call her. Not yet anyway. She was my boss, after all, and I was going to need some time off work in order to help Mom and Dad, so I'd have to call her eventually.

Christopher broke the silence. "I'm going to go grab some coffee. Do either of you want anything?"

I shook my head without looking up, then

Boone cleared his throat. "I might come with you and grab one. I need to make some calls to make sure everything is covered back at my ranch."

Wincing at the fact I'd pulled him away from his animals and chores, I glanced up to his face. "Thank you for coming with me. I know how busy the ranch is at the moment—"

He cut me off with a short, gentle kiss. "Darlin', I wouldn't be anywhere else. I'll just give Liam a call. He'll be fine to take care of everything that needs doing tonight."

He gave me another light kiss before he moved to stand. "Be back before you know it, sweetheart."

Boone

While I did need to let Liam know I would be away for a while, the real reason I wanted to get out of there without Gabs was because Christopher had given me a look that said he needed to talk to me. I doubted he wanted to give me the usual big brother threat of "don't you dare hurt my sister." At least, I hoped he wasn't going to waste time with that bullshit.

"Thanks for following my lead on that,"

Christopher said as we made our way down the hallway. "Look, I'm not sure how long you and Gabs have been together, but her reasons for not calling Silk are bullshit. Those two have been inseparable since they were teenagers. Deep down, I know Gabs wants her best friend here, but for some reason, doesn't feel like she can call her."

I wasn't sure where Christopher was going with this. "So, what are you saying? You want me to get hold of her phone and call Silk for her? Not sure I want to break her trust like that, to be honest. We've only known each other a month and this thing between us is still new. I really like your sister and don't want to ruin it before it has a chance to be something more."

He nodded. "I can respect that. I think I still have her phone number somewhere. I'll give her a call and let her know."

With that, we continued to the cafeteria to get coffees. I also grabbed a bottle of water for Gabs, along with a few packets of chips and M&Ms, in case she got hungry later. While I waited in line to pay, I gave Liam a quick call and explained what was going on. After he assured me he had it all under control and I could focus on Gabs, I hung up and paid for my stuff.

Christopher and I started to make our way

back to the waiting room and I figured I might as well let my parents know what was going on while I had a few minutes. My dad was retired now, so he should be able to head over to help Liam if I needed him to.

"Boone? Honey, what's wrong that has you calling so late?"

Yep, that was my ma, cutting straight to the point.

"I'm fine, Ma. But the lady I'm seeing, well, her parents were in a nasty car accident today and I'm at the hospital with her. I was wondering if Dad would be able to help Liam out over at the ranch? Not sure how long for at this stage. Oh, and of course, you, Summer, and the girls are welcome to head over there too."

"I'm sure he'll be able to get over there to help Liam. Now, I had no idea you had a new lady friend. How long have you been keeping this from your mother?"

That made me smile. It was never a good idea to try to keep anything from my mother. She didn't handle being out of the loop well at all.

"Ma, I wasn't hiding anything, promise. I only met her a month ago. It's all very new still."

"Okay, son, I believe you. Now, you go take care of her, and your father and I will help Liam get everything taken care of out at your ranch."

"Thanks, Ma."

I ended the call and glanced over at Christopher who was still on his phone. From what I could hear of his conversation, he was talking to Gabs' friend, Silk. I wasn't sure if Gabs was going to be happy or pissed off with her brother about calling her friend, but time would tell because from what he was saying, she was on her way here.

I headed back into the waiting room. Gabs was pacing, her arms wrapped around her middle. My heart hurt watching her lost in her misery. I strode over, and after depositing my coffee and the snacks on the table, went to her. Catching her wrist, I pulled her against me so I could wrap her up in my arms.

"It'll all work out, sweetheart. Gonna be hard for a while, but you'll get through it all. I'll make sure of it."

She relaxed against me and slipped her arms around my waist, holding on to me as tightly as I was her. I loved that she found peace with me. I wanted to be that for her. Her anchor in the storm.

I pressed a kiss to the top of her head, silently sealing my promise to her.

As much as we hadn't physically seen each other for the month between us meeting and today, all the phone calls and texts had meant we'd gotten to know each other and I knew if we got the chance, we could have something special. With how long her folks were going to need her attention and focus, it would be some time before we'd get a chance to get intimate, but I was more than happy to wait for my silver-haired beauty. She was worth it.

Gabs

I was still clutching Boone when the door swung open, and a doctor came through. I turned to watch as he went over to the other couple who were waiting in the room with us and delivered his news. They spoke too softly for me to hear what was said, but the woman's tears seemed like relieved ones. At least that was what I was telling myself.

A few minutes later, another doctor came in along with a nurse, and Christopher stood as they headed in our direction.

"Your mother's awake and has been moved to a room. We successfully got her shoulder back in place from the dislocation. She also had a deep laceration to her right forearm that we closed. Time will tell if she suffers any nerve damage from that. We found where she was bleeding in her abdomen and got that taken care of. I'll be by to check on her in the morning and I'll answer any questions you have then. In the meantime, Gemma, here, will take you both to her."

Christopher shook his hand and thanked him. After he left and we followed Gemma out of the room, I turned to Christopher.

"Why couldn't he tell us more now?"

"The pile-up was nasty, Gabs. Lots of injuries on top of two fatalities at the scene. He's going to scrub up to do the next surgery. There are a lot more people to save other than our folks."

Heat flashed over my cheeks that I didn't think of that myself.

"What about you? Should you be in surgery?"

"Once I check in with Mom, I'll have to head off to get scrubbed in. It's going to be a long night."

"You'll make sure someone comes to let us know what's happening with Dad, right?"

He reached over and gave my shoulder a short squeeze.

"Of course, Gabs. You'll probably know before I do."

I scoffed at him, not believing that for a

moment, but before I could say anything to call him on it, we entered a double room where Mom lay still in a bed. She looked so fragile, the sight causing me to stumble a little. Boone was there with an arm around my waist to keep me steady. He didn't say a word, but he didn't need to. Simply having his strong presence there helped so much.

Christopher walked ahead of me and leaned in to press a kiss to Mom's cheek.

"Hey, Mom, how are you feeling? Scared the hell out of us all today."

She gave him a weak smile. "Sorry, son. I'm feeling pretty groggy, but I'll take that over the pain. Where's your father?"

Christopher winced. "Dad's still in surgery, Mom. His leg was badly damaged, but we haven't heard any news on how it's going yet. I promise they'll be in to let you and Gabs know as soon as they can. And I pulled some strings so you'll both be able to share a room once he's out of recovery."

At the mention of my name, she turned from Christopher to look at me with another slight smile.

"My girl, I didn't see you hiding over there."

"Hey, Mom."

I rushed forward and kissed the opposite cheek from the one Christopher had kissed. I wanted to wrap my arms around her and give her a hug, but I couldn't without moving her and potentially causing her pain. Her right shoulder was bandaged, and the white gauze continued down her arm until it disappeared under the sheets.

"Who's with you, sweetheart?"

Boone came up behind me, resting his palms on my waist and pulling me back against him.

"This is Boone, Mom."

"Hello there, Boone. It's lovely to meet you, even if the timing isn't the best."

"Evenin', ma'am."

He didn't say anything more. Poor man was probably looking to escape by now. Our first sort-of date, and it ended with him getting to meet my whole family and deal with medical drama. Fun times, right there.

I prayed it wouldn't scare him off.

Chapter Seven

Boone

I WASN'T sure if it was the drugs or if Gabs' mom normally favored her son over her daughter. The way, when we'd all walked in together she instantly focused on Christopher, not even realizing Gabs was in the room, left me frowning and not exactly jumping at the chance to interact with the woman.

After Christopher headed off to return to work, I pulled over a second chair and sat beside Gabs as she held her mother's hand while chatting to her about random stuff until the woman nodded off to sleep. She had to be on some serious painkillers, which hopefully explained her moment of tunnel vision when we'd first come in. At least, I hoped it was not how she normally treated her daughter.

Gabs didn't say a word to me about it,

even after her mother fell asleep, so I didn't bring it up either. Last thing I wanted to do right now was to add to her stress.

With a sigh, Gabs sat back into her chair and reached for my hand, which I readily gave her. She wrapped both of hers around mine and I leaned over to press a kiss to the top of her head as she rested against my shoulder.

"I got you, sweetheart. Rest while you can."

It was a little awkward in the hard plastic chairs since I couldn't wrap my arm around her like I had in the waiting room earlier. She shifted, keeping my hand clasped in one of hers, and with a deep sigh, relaxed against me and dozed. As she slept, I leaned my head back against the wall and closed my eyes.

The sound of a man clearing his throat had me jerking awake, which in turn woke Gabs and left us both blinking up at the doctor waiting for our attention.

"Oh, sorry! I didn't think I'd be able to sleep, but I guess I was more tired than I thought."

Gabs spoke in a rush as she stood up. The doctor was on the younger side, maybe early thirties, and he looked damn tired, like he'd had an even longer day than Gabs and I had.

"That's quite okay, ma'am. Trust me, I

completely understand having to grab some sleep when you can. Are you related to Mark Rayne?"

"Yes, sir. I'm Gabriela Rayne, his daughter."

I could tell she wanted to ask for news on her father, but the words got caught behind a small sob. I moved to stand behind her, pulling her back against me so I could wrap my arms around her waist. My girl was breaking my heart tonight.

"Your father is out of surgery and is in stable condition."

"What about his leg?"

"Your father's leg was severely damaged in the crash. His left tibia was shattered, and the fibula broken in three places. But we did manage to save the limb. We needed to insert steel rods into his leg. It'll be a long recovery for him."

She slumped back against me in relief. "But he's still got both of his legs."

The doctor nodded. "Yes, ma'am, he does."

"Thank you, so much. Do you know when he will be out of recovery?"

I rubbed my palms up and down her arms as the doctor shook his head.

"I can't give you an exact time, I'm sorry."

With that, the doctor left, and Gabs turned

around and buried her face into my shirt, her body shaking with her sobs.

"Shh, darlin'. I got you."

What else could I say? Her father was damn lucky the doctors had managed to save his leg by the sounds of it, but she already knew that.

She shuddered one last time then pressing her palms against my torso, pushed herself back and looked up at me. Her red-rimmed brown eyes broke my heart. I'd give anything to be able to fix all this for her and see her smile.

"Thank you for being here. For staying. I know you have ranch stuff you probably should be doing right now, and we haven't known each other that long but—"

Cradling her jaw in my hands, I pressed my thumb over her lips, silencing her.

"Gabs, I'm here and I'm not going anywhere. Liam and my father will take care of the ranch while I'm gone. Yeah, this thing we have is new, but it's strong. I already care about you a whole lot, so this is where I want to be—with you, helping you however I can. Okay?"

I shifted my thumb and kissed her. Her hands tightened on my shirt, and she pressed her hips against mine, making my already hard dick throb for more of her. I couldn't believe we hadn't gotten naked together yet. I'd hoped tonight would end that way, but unfortunately life had other plans for our evening.

A loud knock came on the door. She jerked away from me with a gasp. I grinned as her cheeks flashed red and her eyes opened wide before she spun to face whoever it was that busted our heated kiss.

Gabs

Boone melted my heart with his words and his kisses. I couldn't wait to see how explosive we'd be between the sheets, but it appeared the universe didn't want us to go there just yet. Cockblocked by a car crash… It was different, that was for sure.

I'd fully sunken into his kiss, allowing him to carry me away from my injured parents and this whole situation when a knock on the door frame had me jerking away from him. Guilt ate at me that I'd been busted making out like a randy teenager in my mother's hospital room, of all places.

"Damn, girl. You've been keeping all sorts of secrets lately, huh?"

I turned to face Silk as she entered the

room. I hadn't called her. How did she know I was here?

"I didn't realize your brother still had my number. Guess it's a good thing I haven't changed it in the last few years, huh? Or I wouldn't know my best friend needed my ass. Seriously, Gabs, what gives?"

I wasn't sure what to say exactly. Silk and I had been drifting for a long while now. Her life had gotten busy, and changed direction, while mine had stayed the same.

"The doctor was just in here. They managed to save Dad's leg. It got smashed up pretty bad."

I went with ignoring the elephant in the room and moved along to more pressing matters.

Avoidance for the win.

Silk slowly nodded. "And your mom?"

She turned to look at my still sleeping mother.

"She dislocated her shoulder and cut up her arm, but she'll be fine."

Shifting her attention back to me, Silk held my gaze for a minute of awkward silence before she shook her head and strode the rest of the way to me. She set a large Sonic cup on the table before she pulled me from Boone to wrap me in a hug.

"Wish you'd called me sooner. I would

have been here to hold your hand while you waited for news. Brought you a Vanilla Coke from Sonic. Extra-large with a double pump of vanilla."

That made me smile. I loved that drink, but we didn't have a Sonic in Bridgewater, so it wasn't often I got one. Commercial Vanilla Coke just wasn't the same.

"Sorry, Silk. Assumed you'd be busy with Raven and Eagle and stuff…"

My words trailed off.

"Seriously? That's what you going silent on me lately has been about?" Silk took my face between her palms and locked her pale blue gaze onto mine. "No matter what happens, you are my best friend. I'll always make time for you. Yeah, I don't get as much sleep now with a baby and spend half my life wondering where the fuck I left my sanity, but you and me? We'll always have each other."

Tears dripped down my cheeks and she released my face to give me another tight hug.

"Damn it, Gabs. I've missed you."

"We've been working together this whole time, Silk. I didn't go anywhere for you *to* miss me."

"Bull-fucking-shit, you didn't. You've not told me a damn thing in months. Like who's this sexy cowboy who looks like he's trying to decide if I need to be kicked out or welcomed in?"

I chuckled, although it sounded a little watery through my tears. Releasing Silk, I reached for Boone, who took my outstretched hand and wrapped his arm around my waist.

"Silk, this is Boone. Boone, Silk."

Boone gave her a head tilt. "Ma'am."

After running her gaze over Boone, she smirked at me. "That's all the info you gonna give me? Seriously? Fine." She turned to Boone. "Where'd you meet my girl?"

Boone cocked an eyebrow at her. "I met *my girl* a month back at The Barn. Any more details than that, you'll need to ask Gabs."

When he pressed a kiss to my temple, I leaned into him with a smile. I was quickly becoming addicted to how this man made me feel.

"Which I might leave and give you a chance to do," he said. "If that's okay with you, Gabs? I'll head home and double check everything before coming back in. Want me to stop by your place? Grab a change of clothes for you or anything else?"

I rested my palm over his heart and pressed a kiss to the corner of his mouth.

"You are the sweetest man I've ever met. Not sure I want your first time seeing my place to be without me there, or before I've had a chance to clean it up."

He chuckled and the sound vibrated down my spine. "Guess I'll leave that to Silk then. So, you'll be okay if I'm gone for a few hours?"

I ran my gaze over his face. No doubt he'd been up since before dawn working, and it was now past midnight. Exhaustion was showing in the lines on his face and the set of his shoulders.

"I'll be fine. Silk's here with me and Christopher's somewhere close too. But will you be okay driving that far on your own when you're so tired?"

He squeezed me tighter. "I'll grab another coffee to go on my way out. I'll be fine, and I'll be back before you know it."

I reached up and ran my fingers down the side of his face, scraping my nails through his blonde scruff.

"You might as well crash for a few hours in your own bed. Come back in the morning."

He silently watched me. "You sure you don't want me back sooner?"

I didn't want him to leave, but I could hardly tell him that. We'd only known each other for less than a month. Didn't seem right how much I needed him close to feel safe already.

"There's no point in us both not getting any sleep. At least I'm small enough to fit on the couch to maybe get a little."

He gave me a slow nod. "Okay, then. I'll return in the morning. I'll be sure to bring you a Vanilla Coke too, now that I know your addiction."

I laughed. "It has to be Sonic, though. They do something special to theirs."

He gave me another kiss, wiping my mind of all thought, before he pulled back and with a tilt of his head to Silk, sauntered away.

"Hot damn, Gabs. That man is smoking hot and so into you."

I nodded numbly as I stared out the empty doorway. "That he is. Struggling to believe he's real with how great he's been today."

Silk crossed her arms over her chest. I was in for it.

"So, spill. What were you doing up at The Barn when you met your hot cowboy and why haven't I heard one word outta you about him?"

I shrugged as I went over to my mom's bed and fussed with the corner of the sheet.

"I went to The Barn for a drink a month back and we met there. He's a rancher and has been busy with calving so today was the first time we'd been able to line up seeing each other again."

"And instead of a perfect first date, you get to hang out in a hospital. I'm sorry, Gabs."

A small smile crept across my lips at the memory of earlier this afternoon. "Got to help him pull a calf first before I got the call about the accident."

Silk chuckled. "Only you'd be smiling at the memory of something that gross."

"It wasn't gross. Well, there was some blood and other crap, but it was mostly sweet, helping the mama cow birth her calf then watching as she cleaned it up and checked it over."

"Found your match then, huh? Tell me, does he have horses?"

Heat raced over my cheeks as I cleared my throat. "Of course, he does. We were on horseback when we found the mama cow in trouble. He has a stallion and two mares. The mares are rescues."

Silk groaned. "Rescues? Oh, man, could he be any more perfect? Just promise me you'll be careful. Don't rush in and let him trample your heart."

I rolled my eyes. "It's taken us a month to get from meeting to a first date. I think it's safe to say we're taking our time."

Before she could say anything else, her phone rang and when she answered it, I could tell it was Eagle on the other end of the line.

Then the door opened, and a flurry of activity followed as my dad was moved into the bed beside my mom. I had all the distractions I needed to ensure I wasn't going to get caught up thinking about the situation with Silk or Boone.

Chapter Eight

Boone

MY GIRL WAS RUNNING herself into the ground and I couldn't stand by and do nothing. For the last four days, she'd done everything she could to help her folks as they began to recover from their injuries. She'd cleaned their house and brought clothing to the hospital they could wear around their various casts and bandages.

She'd stayed in their room, refusing to go home to rest at night. Curled up on the couch wasn't allowing her to sleep properly, so today I was aiming to fix that. Waiting until she was busy helping her mom, I slipped out into to the hallway and pulled out my phone. I'd grabbed her brother's number earlier in the week and put it to use now.

"Hello?"

"Hey, Christopher, Boone here."

"Oh, hey, man, everything all right with my folks?"

I winced that he not only didn't ask about Gabs, but seemingly didn't know what was going on with his parents—who were staying in the same damn hospital where he worked. I was starting to get a pretty clear picture of how this family functioned, and it wasn't pretty.

"They're the same. I'm calling about Gabs. She needs a break before she falls over. Are you able to come sit with your folks today, so I can take her away for a few hours at least?"

He scoffed. "She understands they're in the hospital, right? Surrounded by doctors and nurses. She doesn't need to be there twenty-four seven. Just take her away. They'll be fine."

Wishing I could reach through the phone to shake the man, I bit back my growl and forced my voice to remain calm.

"Christopher, can you please do this for your sister? Just come down here and sit with your parents while I make sure she gets some rest today."

Another scoff came across the line. "That's bullshit. You just wanna get some from my sister and she won't go with you. Ever think maybe she doesn't like you as much as you want her to?"

My vision went red as I stopped holding back and growled at Gabs' asshole brother.

"You better watch your damn mouth, boy. Don't think I haven't seen how your family works this past week. Everyone leans on Gabs, expects her to do every-fucking-thing without complaint. And she has done just that. For four fucking days she's given her all. She's worn out. If she doesn't get some decent sleep and rest soon, she's gonna be in a damn hospital bed herself. If you don't believe me, get your ass down here and you'll soon see for yourself. Then while you're here, you can man the fuck up, and take your turn with your folks."

I hung up the phone before he could respond and paced the hallway, trying to vent my anger before going back to Gabs. I hadn't lied to the man. She was close to exhaustion. Wanting to take care of her had nothing to do with the sexual desire I felt for her. Did I want her? Definitely. Could I wait for her? Hell, yes.

"Boone?"

Gabs' soft voice had me turning to where she stood in the doorway of her parents' room. I strode over to her.

"Hey, darlin', everything all right?"

With a frown, she nodded. "Are you doing

okay? If you need to head back to your ranch, you can. I totally understand you having things to do."

I pulled her into my arms and held her tightly against me. I doubted Gabs had ever demanded anything for herself. She just kept on giving to everyone around her.

"I'm right where I wanna be, Gabs. But I'm getting worried about you. You need a break."

She shook her head before leaning up to press a kiss to my lips.

"My folks need me here."

With that, she turned and slipped back into the room. Before I could follow her, I caught sight of her brother striding down the hallway. The bastard had been in the building but hadn't even checked in with either his sister or folks this morning? He couldn't have been so damn busy that he didn't have time to look in on his family.

Christopher didn't say a word as he passed me, but he didn't make eye contact, either. That was fine with me. I couldn't think of a damn thing to say to him that wouldn't lead to me wanting to knock some sense into him.

Keeping my eye on him to gauge his reaction, I followed him into the room. He stopped just inside the door and watched as his sister flittered around the room adjusting pillows, straightening out blankets. Basically, doing whatever she could to make both their parents more comfortable.

He turned to me and the look in his eyes gave me hope he was finally seeing that his sister was wearing herself out, that he needed to step the hell up. With a nod, he turned back toward Gabs and moved over to her.

"Hey, Gabs."

"Oh, hey, Christopher. I didn't hear you come in. You get a break in your schedule?"

He nodded and I held my breath, waiting to see where he was going to go with this conversation. I had no clue about his work schedule. He might not be able to spend the entire afternoon with his folks, but if he was working here at the hospital, he could pop in between patients or whatever it was he did here.

"Something like that. Look, sis, you need to get out of here for a while—"

She shook her head, cutting him off. "No, I have to stay here. What if something happens?"

He settled his palms on her shoulders.

"Gabs, they're in the hospital. They're being checked on regularly and I promise, I'll spend all my down time in here with them. I don't have much on my plate today, so I'll be able to be here for most of the day. Go with Boone and get some sleep. You're not going to be much good to Mom and Dad if you're in the bed next to them with exhaustion."

She flipped her gaze from Christopher to me, and I gave her a gentle smile and nod. I'd always take care of her.

Gabs

Christopher nudged me in Boone's direction. Boone took my hand in his and led me through the door, heading out of the hospital.

Blinking against the bright sunshine, I shielded my eyes. "Where are we going?"

"To a hotel. You're going to take a nice, long shower or a bath, if you prefer. I'll order up some room service and once you're done in the bathroom, I'm going to make sure you eat a full meal, then I'm going to tuck you into bed."

I opened my mouth to give him some smartass line about getting me into bed, but I stopped short. The thought of a hot shower and some food that didn't come from a vending machine or hospital cafeteria actually sounded pretty damn good. I couldn't even pretend to myself that I wasn't tired as all get out. The few hours I'd managed to get on the couch in the corner of the room weren't enough to keep me firing on all cylinders.

"Okay."

He paused and glanced over at me with a raised eyebrow, making me frown.

"What? I don't always argue."

"I know, darlin'. It's just if I'd known it would be this easy to get you away from the hospital for a few hours, I would have done it days ago."

I gave him a sad smile. "I would have fought you on it a few days ago. Now, I'm just so tired I don't have the energy to do much of anything. Speaking of which, how far away is this hotel of yours?"

My feet had been aching before we left the hospital.

"Just up the end of this block." He pointed to the building in question. "See it? It's not far, but if you need me to, I can carry you."

He wriggled his eyebrows as he'd finished speaking and I couldn't help but chuckle.

"I think I can make it, but thanks for the offer."

With a nod and smirk, he guided me down the street and into the hotel. As he led me across the lobby, it became clear he'd already booked everything before he'd gotten me out of the hospital.

As we moved toward the elevator, I spoke up. "So, you were confident in me agreeing to leave with you, then?"

He shrugged. "You needed a break, time to relax and recharge your batteries. I intended to keep at you all day until you caved in and came with me, even if it was only to shut me up."

My heart melted. He cared so much for my well-being, he had been willing to piss me off to achieve his goal of getting me to allow him to pamper me for a while. Once we were in the elevator, I tugged on his arm until he turned and looked down at me, an eyebrow raised in question. Wrapping my free hand around his neck, I pulled his face down toward me so I could press my lips to his. With a groan, he released my hand and cupping my face, deepened the kiss.

The ding of the elevator had us pulling apart but not moving. The doors began to close, and Boone swung out his arm to halt them. Wrapping an arm around my waist, he ushered me out of the elevator and down the hallway. Floating in a daze, I stayed silent as he swiped a keycard over the reader and opened the door. He dumped the keycard on the table as I closed the door. Before I could turn, he grabbed me, spun me around, and pressed me against the wall.

"I've missed you, darlin'. I need a little more sugar before I let you go take your shower."

His lips were on mine again, silencing any response I might have. It seemed nuts he'd missed me when we'd seen each other every day, but it turned out, I'd been missing him too. Merely seeing each other hadn't been the same as spending time together. I'd missed his kisses, his touch.

His love.

Did he love me? Was that what this was?

I gently pushed his chest until he broke the kiss and pulled back enough that I could look up into his gaze, searching. His baby blue eyes were still as gorgeous as they'd always been to me, and in them I could see the desire he felt for me, the lust. But what about love? Was it really there, or did I just want to see it?

"C'mon, Gabs. Let's get you into the shower and fed before you fall over."

Letting him believe I was simply tired and not trying to figure out if he was my one-and-only, I allowed him to guide me to the bathroom as guilt weighed me down that I'd been worrying about something so silly when my parents were still back at the hospital. I shouldn't have left. What if something happened?

"Christopher is there with them, and they're surrounded by doctors. They're safe and taken care of, Gabs. Let me take care of you."

Had I spoken aloud?

"You didn't say anything, darlin', but I can guess why you're frowning like you are. I get it. I'd be worried as hell in your shoes too, but if you fall over with exhaustion, you're not going to be any good to them."

With a nod, I didn't bother trying to say anything. He was right. Just like Christopher had been right earlier. With a kiss to my temple, he placed my backpack that I hadn't realized he'd grabbed from the hospital room next to the sink.

"Take your time, Gabs. I'll be waiting for you when you get done."

With that, he turned and closing the door gently behind him, left me alone in the bathroom.

Chapter Nine

Boone

While Gabs showered, I paced the room. What the hell had gone through her mind when she'd broken our kiss? She'd looked into my eyes like she'd been searching for the answer to the meaning of life. Had she seen how much I was falling for her? How I was already over half in love with the woman who I hadn't even seen naked yet?

It was crazy. I'd never waited this long to take a woman to bed. It wasn't like I was waiting on purpose now, life just kept getting in the way of us getting any alone time.

The big bed caught my gaze. Would today be the day we finally got to have sex?

I shook my head. That wasn't what today was about. I needed to bank my desire to get inside her every way I could. The fact I wanted to own her body, mind, and heart wasn't what I should be focused on. I needed to concentrate on taking care of her, getting her rested up and ready to deal with her folks again.

After scrubbing a hand over my face, I stared out the window at the cloudy sky as I listened to the shower running. I'd never had a woman tie me in knots the way Gabs had. I'd had my share of lovers, but never had a woman engage my heart the way Gabs did. Hell, this was the first time I'd been away from my ranch this long since I'd bought the place twelve years ago. I was glad I could trust Liam and my dad to keep things running, although I was sure I'd be hearing about it for a good long while from my father. He never did like calving season.

The water cut off, and I turned toward the table that held the phone and other crap. I hadn't asked her what she wanted to eat, so I ordered a few different things that wouldn't take them long to make. I'd eat whatever she didn't want. I had thought about ordering earlier but hadn't wanted the food to go cold so figured a short wait after her shower was the better option.

With a click, the bathroom door opened, and my breath caught at the sight she made stepping out into the room. She'd changed into form-fitting leggings and a loose, long sleeve top. She looked ready to climb into bed as far as I was concerned, and I wanted nothing more than to do just that alongside her.

"Feel better?"

She gave me a shy nod and I couldn't resist her when she looked so damn adorable. With a few long strides, I was standing in front of her. I wrapped a hand around the back of her neck, pulling her in so I could take her mouth with mine again. I'd missed kissing her this week.

Seeing her every day but not getting any alone time with her had been damn hard, especially when she was stressed most of that time and I wanted nothing more than to pull her into my arms so I could kiss away all her worries.

Her fingers dug into my pecs, and I deepened the kiss, enjoying the hell out of how she moaned and wriggled against me. Not wanting the moment to end, I kept kissing her, running my hands down her sides to caress her hips and waist.

I couldn't get enough of this woman. I wanted her naked and beneath me. Wanted to run my lips over every inch of her sweet skin.

A knock on the door had me jerking away from her with a curse.

"Dammit, I swore I wasn't going to be all over you today. You need to rest. That'll be our food."

After pressing a soft kiss to her forehead, I forced myself to release her and headed over to the door, kicking my own ass the entire way.

After thanking and tipping the man who'd brought up our food, I shut the door and turned my attention back to Gabs. She was peeking under the lids of the various dishes.

"You ordered so much food!"

I shrugged. "Wasn't sure what you wanted. I ordered whatever I thought they'd be able to make quickly when you finished your shower. Take what you want, and I'll eat whatever's left."

She paused with her hand hovering near a steaming plate of creamy pasta and looked over at me.

"There's nothing here you ordered just for you? Like your favorite thing in the world to eat."

Of course, I'd ordered things that had appealed to me and that I thought she'd like, but I wouldn't ever take food from her hand.

"I'm a country boy, darlin'. I'll eat just about anything." I nodded to the plates. "Take what you want, then while you nap, I'll eat whatever you leave. Or order more if I have to. It's all good, Gabs. I'm here to make sure you don't have to worry about a damn thing today, okay?"

Her eyes glazed over with tears, but she didn't let them fall. She cleared her throat and looked down as she took the pasta and a fork before moving to sit cross legged on the bed. Leaving her to it, I headed to the bathroom to give us both a break from me staring at her. I prayed when she woke from her nap later, she'd be willing to stay here a little longer to spend some time with me, although I doubted I'd be that lucky. Once she had a nap, I imagined she'd be hell bent on getting back to the hospital and her folks.

But a man could hope.

Gabs

After having a hot shower, an even hotter make out session with Boone, then eating my fill, I was more tired than I could ever remember being before. I hadn't fought Boone when he scooped me up in his arms, pulled the blankets back, and tucked me in under them. His scruff tickled my skin as he pressed a kiss to my forehead and told me to sleep well. It was to the sound of him quietly finishing off the food that I drifted off into a blissful sleep on the soft, comfortable bed, secure in the knowledge he'd keep me safe while I did.

When I woke, it was to discover I was snuggled up against Boone. Blinking my vision clear, I was careful not to jostle him and wake him up. His Stetson sat on the nightstand and in his sleep, his hair had gotten mussed up. The blonde curls were due for a trim, but I rather liked the slightly shaggy look. The scruff along his jaw was bordering on being classed as a beard and had a little more ginger in it than his hair. I wanted to run my nails through it, then trace a fingertip down his straight nose. And those lips… those soft, talented, wonderful lips of his. I really wanted to kiss them.

But I shouldn't. I should let him sleep. He'd been by my side all week. He'd gone home at night to sleep but had returned each morning and spent all day watching me flit around doing what I could for my folks. I could barely believe how great he'd been.

My bladder was letting me know it needed some attention, so I slipped off the bed, careful to not wake him.

Once I got done with my business and washed my hands, I brushed my teeth and my hair, smiling that Bo had remembered to grab my bag for me. He was such a doll.

When I slipped out of the bathroom, he was still asleep. On top of the covers wearing nothing but his jeans, he made a sight. His arms were muscular, one covered with a full sleeve of biomechanical ink. It was a spectacular piece and one day I intended to sit down and examine every inch of it. But right now, the rest of his body lay spread out for my viewing pleasure. His chest and abs were ripped, but not in a bulky, gym-junkie way. My man was sculpted from hard work and healthy living. A nice dusting of hair across his chest trailed down to the waistband of his jeans.

Pulling my lower lip in between my teeth, I wondered if I shouldn't make the most of our time in this hotel room. I should be getting back to my parents, but Christopher was with them, and it would be such a waste not to take advantage of this opportunity. After all, when would we next get a chance like this? My mom would be released before my dad, and once she was, I'd be even busier trying to keep them both looked after. It could be weeks if not months before we had another opportunity, and I wanted to know what it felt like to have Bo take me, to have him deep inside me. To stare into his baby blues while we came together.

"Like what you see, darlin'?"

Oh, his drawl was even sexier when it was rough with sleep.

Unable to form words, I gave him a mumbled, "Uh huh."

His lips kicked up into a grin as he shifted his arms so his hands were behind his head. My gaze zeroed in on his bulging biceps.

"Got any plans to do anything about it?"

The teasing note in his tone snapped me out of my stupor. Smiling, I reached for the waistband of my yoga pants. With a wriggle of my hips, I shoved them down and off before I glided over to the end of the bed. Keeping my gaze on his, and being as sexy as I could, I lowered my palms to the mattress to crawl over to him.

"Damn, girl."

He reached down and hooking his hands under my arms, lifted me up until our faces were level. My legs slipped to either side of his hips, my breath hitching when his denim-clad erection rubbed up against my panties. I shuddered as he cupped my face and guided me down to his lips so he could kiss me senseless. Dancing my tongue with his, I relaxed and gave over to him, letting every thought other than those about Bo vanish from my mind.

With a swirl of my hips over his hard dick, I had him breaking the kiss with a groan. As he trailed nips and kisses across my jaw, he slipped his hands down my body till he got to the bottom of my shirt. He gathered the fabric in his fists before he began to lift. Sitting up straight, I raised my arms to help Bo get my shirt off. The second he had it raised over my naked breasts—I hadn't bothered with a bra after my earlier shower—I held my breath, nervous about his reaction to my body. He tossed my shirt aside, and I braved looking at his face to see his response since he was being silent.

He grinned like he'd been waiting for me to look at him.

"Gabs, you have to know—I think you're beautiful."

I winced and moved to cover my breasts with my palms. "That's with clothes on. Covering my piercings and ink."

His expression softened as he continued to hold my gaze.

"Only some of them are covered with your clothes, darlin'. I know you have your tongue pierced, and your nose. I've seen all the tattoos on your arms. I can logic it out that you'd have more under your clothes, especially considering what you do for a living. *And* I've felt your nipple rings when you've rubbed up against me. I knew they were there, and I've been dying to see what they look like." He gave me a sexy smirk. "Also curious about where else you might be pierced, darlin'."

I laughed. "Sorry to disappoint, but there's no metal below my belly button."

"Well, damn. Ruined all my dreams, Gabs."

He winked at me before I could get offended and with a laugh, the last of my tension left my body.

Chapter Ten

Boone

THE WOMAN WAS CRAZY BEAUTIFUL, but she thought I was going to reject her because she had some piercings? For her to react like that, some moron in her past must have done just that to her.

His loss.

I wasn't going to make that mistake.

I lowered my gaze from her sweet face and groaned at how pretty her rosy-red nipples looked with the silver bars through each one. On each end of both bars were little lines of gems. I doubted they were real diamonds, but they looked real enough against her nipples. Reaching out, I ran a fingertip over one of ends. The five gems were warm from her skin and when she shuddered at my touch, I kept exploring her jewelry. Gently, I nudged the bar, grinning when her breath caught.

"I'm not sure how much I can mess with these pretty little things, darlin'. I don't want to accidentally hurt you."

She squirmed over me, making my cock throb with need. I wasn't going to last long this first round. I'd waited too long to have her, wanted her too much to go slow.

"You won't hurt me, Bo. As long as you don't try to rip them out or anything crazy, you're good. Just don't stop."

Her last words were on a moan as I gripped both her nipples and tweaked them. When she ground her pussy against my cock, I decided to mix things up. Rolling us over, I pulled her beneath me, so I was over her. I kissed my way down to her breasts and suckled at one as I cupped the other in my palm. Running my tongue around the metal and gems along with the puckered flesh of her nipple, I enjoyed the hell out of the way she squirmed beneath me. When I switched over to her other breast, she threaded her fingers into my hair to hold me to her.

Like I was going anywhere.

I kept teasing her until she was on the edge of coming before I pulled back away from her.

"No!"

She reached for me as I slipped back off the mattress.

"Give me a sec, darlin'. Trust me, I'm not going far."

I undid my jeans and as I tugged them down, the way she undulated and groaned nearly had me coming in my damn pants.

"Fuck, woman. You're temptation itself."

Before returning to the bed, I grabbed my wallet from the dresser and pulled a condom free. When I turned back to the bed, Gabs was watching me with heat in her eyes. Fuck. How the hell had I landed such a sexy, gorgeous woman?

After giving my erection a stroke, I put the condom on and got back onto the mattress.

"I've been wanting you beneath me since that first night, Gabs."

Before she could say anything, I took her mouth with mine, kissing her deeply and thoroughly as I grabbed her leg and lifted it up against my hip. My erection slipped up through her slit, the head bumping her clit and making her throw her head back with a moan, breaking the kiss.

Reaching down, I lined things up and with a slow thrust of my hips, entered her for the first time. Her walls were slick with her arousal, but even so, she was tight. With short, slow pumps, I worked my way deeper as I kissed my way down her neck to tease her breasts and nipples again. Once I had her back up to the edge of an orgasm, I sped up my thrusts, loving how she wrapped her arms around my shoulders as I took us both to the point of no return.

"Boone!"

She went over, her channel squeezing me as I struggled to keep up my strokes into her. A tingle shot down my spine and landed in my balls before I followed Gabs over the edge into bliss. Dropping down onto my elbows, I buried my face in her neck as I caught my breath and tried to get my brain back online. She ran her hands up and down my back, lightly scraping her nails over my skin. I moaned as wicked little aftershocks of my orgasm pinged through my body.

With a reluctant groan, I pulled back, grabbing the condom at the base as I slid from her body.

"That was amazing. Let me just go deal with this."

Climbing off the bed, I stumbled toward the bathroom while I pulled off the condom. I tossed it in the trash and wet a washcloth at the sink before wiping myself down. Once I was clean and had the cloth rinsed out with warm water, I headed back to find Gabs in the exact position I'd left her. She had a sweet, content smile on her lips and her eyes were closed. Unsure if she was asleep again, I lifted her leg so I could clean her up. Her eyes flipped open and watched me.

"You're too good to be true, Bo."

Tossing the cloth toward the bathroom, I slid onto the mattress and pulled her in against me, grinning when she snuggled into my chest.

"I'm nothin' special, darlin'. Just your average country boy."

She scoffed. "Ain't nothing average about you, Bo, and you're no boy."

With a chuckle, I kissed the top of her head and relaxed into the mattress, enjoying simply being able to hold my woman in my arms and praying that sometime soon, I could make it so I'd spend all my mornings waking up just like this.

Gabs

I was dozing off to sleep when my phone rang, and everything came rushing back to the forefront of my mind. How could I be here relaxing and sleeping while my parents were both lying in hospital beds?

Guilt assailed me as I flew from the

mattress over to the desk where my phone was on charge. Seeing the call was from Christopher, I answered it without another thought.

"What's wrong?"

"Whoa, sis. Hello to you, too. Did you have a good rest? Get some food?"

Frowning, I tapped my foot. Why wouldn't he just get on with it and tell me why he'd called?

"Yes, I've eaten, showered, and slept… Now, what's going on? You wouldn't call just to check if I ate or slept."

"Mom's the same, still on the road to recovery…"

He was stalling. He always stalled when it was bad news.

"But? How's Dad?"

"He's back in surgery, Gabs. He had a pulmonary embolism, so they've taken him in for an embolectomy."

I squeezed the bridge of my nose. "English, Christopher. Tell me what happened to Dad in English."

"He had a blood clot reach his lungs and form a blockage. They've taken him into surgery, where they'll put a thin tube into a vein in his arm or thigh, going into his lung to remove the clot."

"A clot. In his lung." I shook my head. "When did he go into surgery?"

"About ten minutes ago."

The math I was doing in my head wasn't adding up to something I wanted to hear, but I couldn't help but ask.

"Why are you just calling me now?"

"Boone was right, sis. You needed some rest, to look after yourself for a while—"

I cut him off. "You weren't there when it happened, were you?"

I never should have left. I was getting enough sleep on the couch in their room to keep functioning. Running off to spend the day with my boyfriend had nearly cost my dad his life.

"Don't bother answering that," I said. "I'm on my way in."

I hung up the phone and reached for my bag. Boone's warm hands slid over my shoulders as he stood behind me. I leaned back toward his warmth before remembering I couldn't give in to his allure.

"I can't. I gotta go."

Pulling free, I snatched up my bag and bolted for the bathroom, where I made fast work of dressing and shoving my hair up into a ponytail. When I came out, Boone was dressed and sitting on the side of the bed pulling on his boots. I refused to notice how down he looked, how his shoulders were slumped, how my brushing him off had hurt him. I had to focus on my parents, not myself. Not the way my heart was tearing apart because I had to give up Boone. He was a distraction I couldn't afford at the moment. My parents' lives were relying on me staying focused on them.

"Boone, you need to stay here. I'll go back to the hospital on my own. I can't do this." I waved a hand between the pair of us. "I can't afford to shift my focus from my parents right now. My dad nearly died because I wasn't there today."

Tears clogged my throat as Boone sprang to his feet and rushed to stand in front of me. He cupped my face, wiping my tears with his thumbs.

"They're in the hospital, Gabs, getting around the clock care. From the part of your conversation I heard, they were watching your dad and got to him in time to save him. You're allowed to take care of yourself too. You're allowed to have a life while they recover."

More tears flowed as I shook my head. The heartbreak in his eyes was nearly more than I could take. With a sigh, he leaned in and pressed a gentle kiss to my lips, then my forehead.

"You change your mind, you know where to find me."

With that, he dropped his hands away and turned for the bathroom, closing the door between us as my heart shattered.

Dashing the fresh tears from my eyes, I tried not to see the mussed-up bed where Boone had made love to me earlier as I quickly gathered my things and stuffed everything into my bag before I slipped out of the door.

Chapter Eleven

Gabs

THE THREE WEEKS following that day in the hotel passed me by in a blur. Dad had thankfully come through the surgery fine, but it had set back his recovery. I continued to stay at the hospital until Mom was released, then I moved back home to make sure she didn't try to do more than she should, and to drive her in to see Dad each day.

Once Dad's condition was more stable, I also went back to Silky Ink. Not full time—Mom needed me during the day—but once she went to bed in the early evening, I was free to head in to work for a few hours.

I was constantly on the move. There was always something that needed to be done, and that suited me just fine. It meant I didn't have time to notice the gaping hole in my heart that Boone had filled. I also didn't have time to give in to Silk, who'd been trying to get me to open up to her about what had happened.

My routine was going to change again today. Dad was finally coming home. Christopher was driving him back. Mom had been fluffing around most of the morning. Her shoulder had healed up, the scar on her forearm was looking good, and it didn't appear she had any long-term nerve damage. However, she still shouldn't be trying to do everything she used to do. She didn't have the energy or stamina she'd had before. Getting her to accept that just because the outside was healing up well, didn't mean internally her body wasn't still trying to recover was a struggle.

I was putting the vacuum cleaner away when a car pulled into the drive.

"Mom? I think that's Christopher with Dad."

She hustled to the front door and swung it open.

"Mom! Slow down, you don't want to re-injure yourself."

She waved me off. "Oh hush, Gabs. I'm fine. It's your father who's going to need fussing over, not me."

Rolling my eyes, I followed her out to greet the men.

Half an hour later, Dad was settled on his recliner in the family room snoring away. Mom was fussing in the kitchen making him something to eat for when he woke up, and Christopher was frowning my way.

"What?"

"When did you last go to your place?"

I shrugged. "Um, I'm not sure. Two weeks ago? Three, maybe. I went and packed up some more clothes and stuff when Mom was released, and I moved in here."

I was not telling Christopher about the eggs that had been smashed against my front door, or how my flower garden under my kitchen window had been ripped up, the flowers tossed all over the place to die. Nope. My brother didn't need to know about any of that.

"And when did you last do something for yourself… that wasn't going to Silky Ink?"

Instantly forgetting all about the issues with my trailer, heat crept up my neck and flashed over my cheeks as I remembered the day Boone had taken me to the hotel. Then my anger kicked in and I turned to glare at Christopher. How dare he make me feel like shit for all I was doing.

In a whisper-yell so I didn't wake up Dad,

I said, "You know *exactly* when the last time was. I haven't had a chance since then! In case you haven't noticed, it's been a full-time job to keep Mom from doing too much. And now with Dad home, it'll be even harder to keep her resting like she should be."

He nodded and the sympathy in his gaze had me wanting to throw something.

"And without Boone around to call us on our shit, we've all sat back and let you do everything again. I don't know what happened that day at the hotel, but I wish it hadn't. He was good for you, Gabs. Hell, he was good for us too." He stood and came over to me, pulling me up from where I was sitting. "Mom's not the only one who needs to be careful to not over-do things. I've taken the next three days off to stay here and help out. How about you go back to your place and relax? Take a bath, read a book, go ride a horse. Whatever it is you need to do, do it. Live a little. And maybe give Boone a call. Whatever happened can't be so bad. Clearly, you were feeling him. I know you've been trying to hide it and all, but I'm your brother, Gabs. I know you. I can see the pain in your eyes."

Shock held me frozen in place. My brother had never spoken to me like that before. I'd actually wondered on occasion if he felt emotions at all, or if he was more robot than man. Emotion clogged my throat as he leaned in to press a soft kiss on my forehead, just like Boone had that final time. I couldn't speak as he pulled back and looked me in the eye.

"Go on home, Gabs. Take a few days to recoup. Mom and Dad are going to need us both for a good, long while yet. Once you get some R 'n' R time, we'll sit down and do up a schedule, yeah? So we get them covered but without working you to the bone in the process."

I nodded, wondering where this new and improved Christopher had come from. Normally, he was totally ignorant to how much I did.

"Thanks for this. It'll be good to go back to my trailer for a bit."

I wouldn't be able to go riding, though. That thought sat like a lump of lead in my stomach as I packed up some of my clothes. Once I had that done, I said goodbye to Mom, telling her to call me if she needed anything. Then, after a quick bye to Christopher, I was out the door and loading my stuff into my car.

It didn't take long to drive back home. Nerves at what I'd find this time had me white-knuckling the steering wheel as I turned into my driveway.

"Motherfucker!"

I rarely swore, but rolling up to find my house with toilet paper wrapped all around it warranted a few curse words. For a few moments, I contemplated turning around and heading to the motel in town but that would be a waste of money. I would need to tidy all this mess up at some point, and it might as well be now.

With a sigh, I got out and headed to the front door, wincing as I got a closer look at all that had been done to my poor little trailer. Not only had there been toilet paper thrown around, but someone had put newspaper over the windows all along the front. I could take a guess that all the windows had been given the same treatment. Why would Royce be this childish? Surely, if he was truly so hurt at my refusal of his advances, he'd just give me an eviction notice, not pull childish pranks.

Sliding the key in the lock, I went to grab the handle but stopped when I saw something covered it. It looked like peanut butter, but I hadn't been home in so long, whatever it had been was now hard and crusty. Not wanting to touch it, I pulled a tissue out of my handbag to cover it before I turned the knob.

Holding my breath, I shoved open the door and relief washed over me when the interior looked as it should. Royce had thankfully kept his games to the exterior.

Making my way through to my room, I set my bag on my bed and opened it up. Taking out my dirty clothes, I put them in the washing machine before I moved to the kitchen. I'd stopped at the grocery store on my way and picked up a few things, so I set about putting them away. Thankfully, when I'd come back three weeks ago, I'd thought to empty out my fridge so there weren't any nasty surprises waiting for me.

Speaking of nasty surprises, it was time to deal with the exterior. Taking a garbage bag, I headed out and gathered up all the toilet paper. The newspaper had dried against the glass and wasn't coming off easily, so I grabbed the hose and wet it all down to let it soak. I then moved onto scrubbing the doorhandle.

By the time I had it all cleaned up, and the paper scraped off the windows, I was more than ready for a shower and a nap. Before I did either, I put the kettle on to boil some water for a cup of tea. While I waited, I looked out the now clean window above the sink and let my mind wander. Since I refused to give Royce another moment of my time, my brain went with thoughts of Boone.

Christopher had no idea what had happened at the hotel. He couldn't. There was no way he could know that it had been my guilt over not being there when Dad had taken that turn that had me sending Boone away. And now it was my cowardice that had me working my ass off so I didn't have time to think about him, about how much I missed him, about how much I wished I could pick up my phone and call him. If I ignored my broken heart for long enough, it'd stop hurting eventually. Right?

Gabs

"What the fuck?"

With her head hanging over the top of the fence, Whiskey stared in through the window at me. I'd never seen her look so miserable and unkept. Instantly, I was furious that Royce had been so busy messing with my house, he'd not bothered to look after the horses he'd banned me from caring for.

I grabbed an apple and chopped it up before I raced outside and climbed over the fence. Whiskey plodded toward me as I rushed to her.

"Hey, girl."

I held out the first chunk of fruit and she scarfed it down like she'd never seen an apple before. I ran my gaze over her body as I continued to feed her the remaining pieces. She'd lost a lot of weight since I'd last seen her, enough that I could see her ribs through her coat. Speaking of her coat, it was a mess, and her tail and mane were a mass of tangles too. She'd clearly not been groomed in a long time. There was also a shallow gash to the side of her chest.

As she ate the final chunk, I stroked down her face, from between her eyes down to her nose. "What's been going on, Whiskey? You're looking damn skinny, girl. How about you show me what's going on back at the barn, yeah? Just let me change my shoes."

Climbing back over the fence, I jogged inside the house and after chopping up another apple, I switched out my shoes for boots, grabbed my hat, and returned to Whiskey. It broke my heart to see her in the condition she was in. If only Royce hadn't been such a dick about things, I would have happily kept looking after all the horses. It would have been a struggle while looking after my parents too, but I would have somehow worked out a way to fit it all in.

Hopping over the fence again, I gave her another chunk before I walked across the field toward where the barn was. Whiskey plodded along beside me, munching on the apple pieces I was slowly feeding her as we walked.

I had no clue what I was going to find once inside. Whiskey looked like she'd been completely neglected for months. The fact it had been two months since I'd last seen any of John's horses had me worried that had been the last time they'd been groomed or fed properly.

As I got closer to the barn, Whiskey slowed down, clearly not wanting to go back inside. I turned toward her and gave her some love, murmuring words of assurance until she seemed calm enough to continue.

"C'mon, girl. I need to check on the others, get you all fed and brushed."

She huffed at me like she didn't fully agree with my plan but tough luck for her because that was what was going to happen. I approached the barn, looking around for any sign of Royce or John. The structure was out of sight from the main house, so when I didn't see anyone, I went up to the door. It had been busted open from the inside. Tears pricked my eyes when I spotted the blood on a splinter, where, no doubt, Whiskey had hurt herself.

"Oh, you poor sweetheart. You broke yourself out, didn't you?"

She nosed my shoulder with a huff. Tears stung my eyes as I forced the broken door to open all the way. The smell of manure was thick in the air, and I coughed as my eyes watered for a different reason other than my emotions.

"Dammit."

The other horses began making noise and stomping their feet, like they were worried I didn't know they were there.

"I'm coming, girls."

I headed into the feed room. There was still plenty of grain and hay. Shaking my head at Royce's stupidity, I turned and went to each of the stalls and collected all their buckets. After washing them out as fast as I could, I hung them and tossed a few flakes of hay into each stall. The urge to feed them grain was strong, but I knew it could harm their digestive system if fed too soon after a bout of starvation.

Whiskey refused to go back in her stall, and since she'd busted the latch on the door, I didn't bother trying to force her in there. Instead, I put her hay and a water bucket out in the main area so she could eat something more filling than a couple of apples.

Once they were all munching on their hay, I set about cleaning their automatic waterers and making sure they were working. Then I picked up a brush and headed back to Whiskey. I was about to start when it occurred to me that I should take some photos for proof. If John was sick or had simply handed over the horses' care to Royce, not realizing how incapable he was, I needed to show him the truth. And if he wouldn't do anything about fixing the situation, I'd call in the SPCA.

Pulling out my phone, I snapped photos of the broken door and gate, then of each of the horses, including a close-up of Whiskey's scratch. Then I grabbed the brush again and started grooming her. Once I had her brushed and her mane and tail detangled, I went back to the feed room and searched for what I needed to deal with her injury.

With a bucket full of water with antiseptic solution in it, along with a packet full of cotton pads, I headed back to her and set about getting the injury cleaned up.

By the time I had all the horses brushed down and released out into the pasture so I could muck out the stalls, I was beyond furious. How dare Royce neglect these animals like he had? Weaved into my fury was worry for John. No way would he ever knowingly allow his animals to be neglected like this.

I needed some advice right now. Simply marching up to the house and raging at Royce wouldn't do a damn bit of good, but if I called in the SPCA, would they just come and seize the animals? John didn't deserve to lose them because he'd trusted his son.

Boone worked for the SPCA. I could call him to get his advice on what to do before making an official complaint. Assuming he'd even answer my call. My pride hadn't allowed for me to try to contact him since that day in the hotel. Guilt over that weighed on me. He deserved better after all he had done. And now I was only calling with something work-related.

I could use this as an excuse to reconnect with him. Not that my relationship with Boone was the priority here, the horses were.

Chapter Twelve

Boone

IT HAD BEEN two months since my silver-haired beauty ripped my heart in two. I'd come home and buried myself in work, which was easy to do during calving season, even if I did have my family underfoot asking questions for that first week or so.

Now calving was just about done, and I had way too much damn time on my hands. I often ended up thinking about Gabs and the short amount of time I'd had with her. Even today, when I was at my parents' place surrounded by family, including my three nieces who wanted me to constantly play hide and seek with them, I couldn't completely push Gabs from my mind.

Mentally shaking my head, I told the girls I needed a breather and headed inside to grab a beer. As I walked up the stairs onto the back porch, my mind kept rolling on the Gabs train, thinking about how if I hadn't stepped in and gotten her out of the hospital that day and forced her to rest and eat, she would have worked herself into the ground. I couldn't help but worry about who was making sure she didn't overdo it now that I wasn't there. I could only hope that after I'd pointed it out to her brother, he paid a little more attention to his sister's welfare.

When I saw both Ma and Summer were already in the kitchen prepping dinner, I made fast work of grabbing a beer from the fridge before either of them could start in on me.

"Hey, bro, my girls wore you out already, huh?" Summer asked as she continued slicing up potatoes.

I took a swig before turning to answer her with a smirk. "They sure did. They gang up, and it's just not fair. I am but one man."

Summer and my mother laughed as I drained half the bottle in a couple swigs.

"Oh, son, don't come at us like that," Ma said. "We all know how much you love those girls."

My mom went silent in the way she did before she'd say something she knew I wouldn't like, which meant it'd be about my lack of providing them with more grandbabies. Thankfully, before she could get started on that line of conversation, my phone rang, saving me.

"Sorry, gotta take this."

Grateful for the reprieve, I didn't check who was calling before I answered as I stepped into the family room.

"Hello?"

"Hey, Bo."

Those two words spoken in that sweet southern drawl made sure the call had my full attention. There was only one person in the world who called me Bo.

"Gabs?"

Silence followed, and I pulled the phone away from my ear to see if the call had dropped.

"Gabs, you there? What's going on?"

She cleared her throat. "Um, well, Dad got discharged from the rehab facility today and Christopher is staying with him and Mom so I could have some down time. Um, you know, so I could have a break. I figured I'd come home for a while. Tidy up, relax. I haven't been home for more than ten minutes since the accident."

Something big had happened for her to be rambling about bullshit like she was, and I was getting worried. "Gabs, darlin', you don't need to tell me how hard you work. I'm well aware. Although, it's nice to hear your brother is stepping up to help out. What's going on? You need help?"

She paused, and my worry for her increased. What the hell could have happened?

"Whiskey was in the field by my house. You should have seen her, Boone. She's so skinny, and has this gash on her chest—"

With that, she had my full attention in a different way. She was well aware I volunteered with the SPCA to help deal with cases of animals in that exact situation.

"You telling me the horse has been neglected? Abused? What about the others? Your landlord had more than one horse, right?"

There was a catch in her voice. "Yes, that's what I'm saying. I followed Whiskey back to the barn. She'd busted her way out of her stall and the barn. That's how she cut herself. All the horses are severely underfed and haven't been groomed in months. I took some photos before I brushed them. I've fed them all, cleaned everything up and tended to Whiskey's cut. They're out in the field now, and I'm in the process of mucking out all their stalls."

Damn, she was one hell of a woman. She'd

seen those horses were in need and took care of it. That endeared her to me all the more, not that I needed more reasons to love her. If only she'd not pushed me away, I would have been with her when she'd found Whiskey in the first place. Owners could get nasty when confronted about their actions, and since she still hadn't told me exactly what she wanted from me, I was worried she'd been hurt.

"Have you spoken to your landlord about it yet?"

"Not yet. I wanted to get the horses looked after first, and I needed time to cool down. Not that time has helped. I'm still so damn furious. I would have been happy to keep looking after them. There was no need for this to happen!"

Relief she hadn't been harmed flowed through me as I wondered exactly how she would have managed to look after the horses when she hadn't even had time to look after herself since the accident, but I kept that to myself. It wasn't going to help anything to bring it up now.

"There's never any need for animal neglect to happen, Gabs. But sadly, it does every damn day of the year. Now, while I'm more than happy to hear from you for any reason, why exactly did you call me?"

She sighed heavily. "I don't know what to

say to Royce or John about this. How do I deal with this in a way that they'll listen? Royce is an ass and clearly still nursing a wounded ego after I shut him down two months back. He mentioned his dad was ill back then, but surely, he can't still be."

This Royce guy sounded like a grade-A asshole. "Gabs, I don't want you going up there by yourself. I'm at my folks' place so can't be there for at least an hour. Is there anyone else you can call to go with you? One of the guys you work with?"

"I'll be fine. Royce is all bark and no bite, always has been. He'd never physically hurt me, however I'm pretty sure he won't listen to me. And those horses mean the world to his dad. I'm worried something's happened to him."

Her flippant attitude toward this man set my teeth on edge. "Don't be reckless around this guy, Gabs. He might be more dangerous than you think. Give me directions and I'll get Liam to come over. I don't want you going up to that house alone."

Silence echoed down the line, and I worried I'd overstepped once again. I wasn't anything to her anymore. She had no reason to listen to me. I was about to have another attempt at convincing her when she spoke.

"Please, Bo, just give me an idea of what to say. That's all I need right now."

I wanted to reach through the phone and shake her. So damn stubborn and independent.

"Gabs, you can lean on me, okay? I know we're technically not together or anything, but I want to help you. Be there for you. I'm concerned about that Royce guy, that you're not taking the threat he poses seriously. If he's willfully neglected those horses like he apparently has, he's not going to have any more respect for human life. He could really hurt you."

"He won't hurt me, Boone. And I'll be careful, I promise."

Realizing she wasn't going to budge on going in alone, I did my best to guide her on what to say.

"All right, just stick with the facts. Lay out that if the horses aren't taken care of, the SPCA will come in. That'll mean fines and potentially the animals being taken away. Even if he doesn't care about the horses, he should care about his bank account. Once you've said your piece, you get out of there."

"I need to head into Silky Ink for a few hours tonight anyway, so no worries there. By the time I get done mucking out the stalls, I won't have much time left before I need to go in."

Closing my eyes, I rubbed the bridge of my nose.

"Can you text me every half hour and again when you get home afterward? Let me know you're all right."

Her voice softened. "I can do that. Thanks, Bo."

She hung up and as I slipped my phone into my pocket, I rubbed the ache in my chest. Damn, I missed her something fierce.

Gabs

Ending the call, I leaned my head against the side of the barn and bit back my sigh. While Boone's protective side was something I liked about him, the last thing I needed right now was to start some kind of Alpha male war between him and Royce. I was grateful he was at his folks' place and too far away to rush straight over here. At least, that was what I was telling myself.

"Men…"

Shaking my head, I set a timer to go off every half hour for the next three hours then got back to mucking out the last stalls. By the time I finished, I'd texted Boone three times. After putting in several large flakes of hay so they could continue to much for several more hours, I got all the horses back in and settled for the night. I even managed to get Whiskey back into her stall, although I couldn't latch her gate shut properly. I hoped she'd stay put until I came back in the morning.

Stroking each of their faces as I closed their stall doors, I spoke to each one.

"I'll be back in the morning. I won't let you suffer anymore."

After closing the broken barn door as best I could, I made my way up the hill to the house. I'd hoped my temper would have cooled off by now, but I wasn't any calmer. There was no need for the horses to get to the point they were. I would have happily kept looking after them.

I was about to climb the front stairs when the sound of an approaching vehicle filled the air. Turning, I saw Royce come flying over the grass toward the house on an ATV. The closer he got, the more of him I could see. I frowned. He was not only covered in dirt but looked tired and worn out.

Royce had never done more than he'd absolutely had to. The fact he'd been clearly out working in the pastures all day didn't make any sense. I just couldn't accept that he would have changed this much.

I didn't say a word until he'd parked and walked over to me.

"Whatcha doing over here, Gabs? Did something break at your place?"

I shook my head, in shock that he'd act like he hadn't threatened me last time we spoke. This wasn't how I'd expected him to behave.

"My place is fine. I'm here because when I got home earlier today, Whiskey was waiting for me."

"Whiskey? A drink was waiting for you? I really don't know what you're on about, Gabs, but I'm too damn tired to deal with it."

Instantly, fury flared through me. My jaw dropped as he stomped past me, toed off his boots, then entered the house.

"What. The. Fuck?"

At my words, he froze part way through the door and turned back to me. Before he could utter a word, I continued, "Whiskey is the name of one of *your* dad's horses. You know? Those beautiful creatures that live down in the barn that you haven't bothered to even look at in a couple of months? Not since you banned me from doing the work. Neglect is animal abuse, Royce. Those horses are starved, and Whiskey hurt herself breaking out to come to me for help. Where's your dad? There's no way he'd let this happen!"

By the time I finished speaking, my voice was loud enough to make my own ears ring a little.

So much for not yelling.

Royce's shoulders dropped and he hung his head. He was being so unlike his usual self, I had no idea what to do with him. I'd expected him to get defensive, to tell me I still couldn't look after them. That he had it all handled because he was a man, while I wasn't. This silence was not the Royce Emerson I knew. Not at all.

"Got any answers for me, Royce? Because you can't continue to ignore them. If your father doesn't want them anymore, sell them. Don't torture them with neglect. It's not fair to them."

With a huff, he looked me in the eye. "My folks are both sick enough I'm having to do all the work around here. It's calving season and I'm busy as fuck dealing with that. Honestly? I forgot all about the damn horses since I don't ride."

Didn't that just say it all? Damn man didn't ride. Grew up on a ranch and was playing rancher now, but he didn't know how to ride a damn horse. I couldn't remember a single time when John had been too ill to take care of the ranch.

"Where are your folks? Are they in the hospital? What's wrong with them?"

He cleared his throat and looked away. "They're still here. It's just the flu or something. They'll be fine soon, I'm sure."

Those horses hadn't been fed in *months*. It couldn't be any simple illness. It also hadn't escaped my notice he was yet to invite me inside. The longer I stayed, the more questions I had. My phone alarm sounded, and I grabbed it out of my pocket to turn off and text Boone to say I was okay.

"If you got somewhere to be, don't let me hold you up."

I took a deep breath as I fought the urge to throw my phone at him. I had to pick my battles. Clearly, he wasn't going to tell me anything more about his folks, but I could help the horses.

"I'm going to be looking after those horses from now on. If you try to stop me, I'll call in the authorities. So, you better call the feed store and let them know I'm allowed to put in orders on your behalf. And if I don't see either of your parents in the next week, I'll be calling in a welfare check on them. If they're that sick, they need to be in the hospital. Bed rest clearly isn't going to be enough for them to recover, Royce."

With that, I had nothing else to say, and didn't want to listen to any more of his bullshit, so I spun on my heel and headed back toward home. As I started walking, I couldn't help but wish I had an ATV right now myself. I was worn the hell out and after the trek home, I still needed to shower before going into work for a few hours.

Chapter Thirteen

Gabs

A WEEK LATER, I was sitting in the break room at Silky Ink, about ready to fall asleep at the table.

With my father home from rehab, I thankfully didn't need to drive Mom into Houston to visit him anymore. While her injuries were mostly healed, the doctor didn't want her doing everything she normally did just yet, so I was still spending a fair amount of time over there. Christopher was thankfully helping out more than he ordinarily would. Guess Dad's embolism was the wake-up call he'd needed. Or maybe Boone had spoken with him, said something before he took me to the hotel.

I mentally shook my head. It didn't matter. Even with Christopher helping out, it didn't ease my load all that much. I was back to working nearly full-time hours. My bills didn't care that I had other priorities lately, and were stacking up. I was also going to the barn twice a day to tend to the horses while avoiding Royce. Despite the fact he said he was too busy to do everything, he managed to find the time to get under my feet, finding me to ask the most basic of questions. It was annoying as hell, and I didn't have time for whatever game he thought we were playing. On the upside, there'd been no more vandalism of my trailer in the past week, which only confirmed my suspicion that Royce was behind it. But I didn't have the energy to puzzle that one out.

That didn't leave much time for anything else, including sleep. Boone and I had texted a couple of times, but there hadn't been any more calls and I hadn't taken him up on any of his offers to help with the horses or anything else.

"Gabs? You in here?"

Silk's softly spoken question jerked me out of my thoughts.

"Yeah."

I lifted my cup of coffee and took a drink as she walked into the break room and sat opposite from me at the table. She was frowning and watching me like I was a high school science experiment that was about to blow up.

"Talk to me, Gabs."

Tears pricked my eyes, and I fought them back. Part of me wanted to crack right open and just let it all pour out at Silk's feet. To share my burden with her. But she couldn't do anything to help. No one could. I was stuck with each of my responsibilities at the moment, so there was no point in stressing her out with my issues.

"About what?"

"The fact you look like you haven't slept in a week, maybe longer. You're burning the candle at both ends and about to run out of wax, babe. Did something else happen with your dad?"

After another mouthful of coffee, I shook my head. "He's still home, slowly getting better."

"Your brother pulling his usual shit and leaving you to do it all?"

That had me smiling. "Surprisingly, he's been helping more than I'd have expected. But he's still putting in long hours at the hospital and can't get down here more than a few times a week."

Silk frowned as I took another sip of coffee. I was delaying the inevitable at this point. There was no putting her off when she got like this.

It was nice to have the old Silk back, even if it was just for a little while, although I wasn't sure where to even start with all that'd gone on lately.

"Gabs, seriously, quit stalling on me. Clearly, something has happened this past week. Has Boone done something?"

My eyes stung again. Silk seemed determined to get me bawling today.

"Boone's gone. I, uh… I broke things off the day they found that embolism in Dad's lung."

She sighed, and I cringed, waiting for her opinion on how stupid I'd been.

"You're set on being an island, aren't you? You can't keep bottling everything up and trying to do everything yourself, Gabs. It's going to destroy you from the inside out. Yeah, I've got Raven and Eagle now, and that takes some of my time, but not all of it. I'll always have time for you. I'll always be here, ready to help. Boone seemed like he could be someone you could count on too. What'd he do that had you pushing him away? Talk to me, Gabs. Let me in, just a little so I can fucking help you already!"

Emotion rose up in me, and I wanted to run away from it. From everything. The last thing I wanted to do right now was discuss how badly I'd screwed up with Boone. I'd sent away a man I was missing like crazy.

Shoving my seat back, I stood and turned to take my mug over to the sink.

"I need to get back to work."

Silk stood and followed me, leaning against the counter beside me. "I know you have at least another twenty minutes before you need to go prep for your next appointment. Enough bullshit. Talk. To. Me."

I wasn't up for talking about Boone, but I could tell her about the horses. Maybe that would be enough to satisfy her.

"Last week, while Christopher was with Mom and Dad, I went home for the first time in ages. Whiskey was waiting for me."

My voice cracked on the last word. I stared down at my hands as I rinsed my mug a second time before drying it, trying to get my thoughts and emotions under control.

"Whiskey?"

She didn't remember the name of my favorite horse. My temper flashed as I remembered how Royce hadn't remembered either.

Putting the mug away, I shook my head. "Don't worry about it, Silk. I got everything covered and things will go back to normal eventually."

I bit my tongue before I threw out that she should just go back to being focused on her man and baby and ignoring me. I knew that was over the line and not fair at all. Silk was trying and I was the one being a bitch, but I couldn't seem to reel it in.

Silk slowly straightened and grabbed my arm before I could leave.

"I do worry, Gabs. Right now, I'm more than fucking worried about you. Tell me what happened. Let me—"

I waved my hand through the air, cutting off her words.

"Just leave it be, Silk. There's nothing you can do, okay? This is just my life right now. It's full on and I'm busy as hell, but it'll pass."

With that, I pulled from her grip and rushed out of the room. In the main room, both SeVen and Donny paused their machines to stare at me with concern but quickly returned to work when I waved them off and headed to the counter. Before I got there, the door opened with a customer. Forcing a smile on my face and my muscles to relax, I switched to work mode and set about booking him in for the piercing he wanted. By the time I'd finished, my next client was waiting. My last appointment for the day. After checking Silk's appointments, I knew she'd be busy with her own client by the time I finished up, so I'd be able to escape without risking another run-in with her.

Deep down, I knew Silk was right. I couldn't keep working myself this hard. Something had to give and soon, or I'd fall in a heap and be the one in hospital, just like Boone had warned me.

The easiest thing to take off my plate was the horses. I couldn't keep being the sole caretaker for them. I needed to carve out some time to look for a long-term solution.

Royce still hadn't allowed me to see for myself how sick John and Kate were, but if whatever they had was something permanent or, heaven forbid, terminal, the horses needed to be rehomed. As much as I was making sure they were fed and groomed, I didn't have time to ride them. It was cruel to lock them up like they were. They were used to being ridden every day and working the ranch.

I could tell they were pining for the action of their previous lives. John had cycled them, taking a different horse out each day to check cattle. All the horses looked so damn sad every time I saw them. They were starting to put a little weight back on, their ribs not showing so obviously anymore, but their eyes revealed their misery. They missed John and the exercise but sadly, there were only twenty-four hours in a day, and none of them were spare for me at the moment.

Boone

Determined to find a way to at least see Gabs, I headed into Silky Ink. I couldn't get her out of my head, and I wasn't willing to just let her go because her life was busy. Now that calving was over, I had a couple of months before I'd get busy again with branding, inoculating, and castrating the males. I wanted to use that time to get my girl back.

When I walked through the door, my heart sank. She wasn't in the main room. Praying she was in a back room or somewhere on the premises at least, I headed straight to the counter.

"Boone? That you?"

Jerking my gaze to the man who'd called my name, I grinned. "Donny! Man, how are you? I had no idea you worked here."

Donny had done my bio metric tattoo for me a few years ago. I'd had no idea he'd moved shops.

"You got time to hang around? I have another twenty minutes or so here, then we can catch up for a bit."

I nodded. "Sure, man. I got time. Is Gabs around?"

He shook his head, "Sorry, buddy. She won't be in till later."

I nodded, trying to cover my disappointment I turned to scan the tattoo designs that hung on the walls of the waiting area. Lost in my thoughts, I started when a female voice quietly called my name.

"Boone?"

I turned to see Gabs' friend, Silk, standing behind me.

"Hey, Silk. What's up?"

She frowned. "I don't know. I was hoping you could tell me."

I glanced around the shop. No one was in earshot, but I still didn't want to be airing Gabs' and my private shit out here.

"Got somewhere more private where we can have a coffee while we chat?"

She nodded. "Come on back to the break room. Donny'll find us when he's done."

I followed her down the hallway and into a small room that held a table and a few chairs, a couple of couches, and a counter along the back wall held a small kitchen area including a fridge and microwave.

"Take a seat," she said. "How do you take your coffee?"

"Black, no sugar."

She nodded and turned to the machine to get it going. I didn't say anything until she'd made both our drinks and came over to sit opposite me at the table.

"I've known Gabs since we were fourteen years old. She's more than my best friend. I consider her a sister. She's always told me everything going on in her life, until now. She seems to have it in her head that now that I have a husband and baby, I don't have time for her." She winced and cleared her throat. "You two seemed close at the hospital, but she told me she broke things off with you. So, why are you here now, and what the hell happened?"

Taking a sip of my coffee, I kept my gaze on Silk, trying to decide how much to tell her. Gabs had to work with this woman, I didn't want to risk making things difficult for her here.

"Why not ask her?"

"I tried. She's being very evasive. She's also about to collapse from working herself to the bone, so I want to know what's going on so that maybe I can help her before she crashes. I'm assuming you want the same thing. Or did you really come in just to see Donny?"

I set my mug down, deciding to go all-in and be completely honest with this woman. It seemed everyone put Gabs second, even Silk, her best friend. I needed to be the one person who would put her first, no matter the cost.

"I didn't even realize Donny was working here before I saw him just now. I came in hoping to catch Gabs since I can't seem to get hold of her any other way. Look, Silk, I don't want to make things harder for Gabs by telling you stuff she doesn't want you to know. What do you know about her and me?"

She sat back, crossing her arms over her chest. "I know you met at The Barn about two months ago. She mentioned something about her helping you pull a calf. And I know that even with all the shit going on with her folks, she lit up when you came back into that hospital room. She needed you there. So, what happened?"

I pinched the bridge of my nose. Figuring she didn't know the full story of the night we'd first met, I left that whole part of things alone and focused on the current situation. "I took her away from the hospital for a day. She was burning herself out, so I got hold of her brother to come sit with her folks, so she'd come with me to a hotel. I made sure she got a shower, food, and some sleep."

I cleared my throat as heat flashed over my cheeks.

Silk chuckled. "I can imagine how she

showed her gratitude after she woke up. I don't need details. How'd it go wrong?"

"Her dad took a turn while she was away from the hospital. Her brother called to tell her, and she told me I was a distraction she couldn't afford and left. Wouldn't even let me take her back to the hospital."

Silk leaned forward, her palms around her mug. "Do you know who, or what, Whiskey is?"

I raised my eyebrow at her, shocked. "If you've been Gabs' best friend since you were teens, how in the hell can you not know the name of her favorite of her landlord's horses?"

"Aw, fuck. I knew it was familiar. Dammit. No wonder she got pissed off at me. I do know, I just forgot. I do have an eight-month-old son that steals my sanity most days. What happened with the horse?"

I paused to stare her directly in the eyes. "You better be as good a friend to her as you say you are. She'll never forgive me if she finds out I told you all this and you use it to hurt her."

Donny clapped me on the shoulder, and I jumped in surprise. I'd been so focused on Silk, I hadn't noticed him enter through the door behind me.

"Normally, the two of them are

inseparable. You can trust Silk with anything you have on Gabs. Honestly, all three of us are worried about her."

He grabbed himself a can of soda before joining us at the table.

"She came to The Barn two months ago to drown her sorrows. Her landlord's son had made a pass at her. When she didn't fall at his feet, he banned her from the barn."

Silk sucked in a breath. "That would have devastated her. Oh, hell, I can't believe she didn't come to me with this shit."

Donny chipped in, "The fact she went to The Barn and not Styx means she didn't want any of us knowing about it."

"After she left me at the hotel," I said, "I didn't hear from her until last week. She'd gone home and Whiskey was waiting for her. She'd been badly neglected, so Gabs followed her back to the barn and after she tended to the horses, she called me for advice. Or to vent, I guess. I was at my folks' place out on the other side of Houston so couldn't go to her. We've had a few texts since then and as far as I can tell, she's now the only one looking after those horses."

Silk sat straighter. "So, she's looking after her folks, the horses, and working here?"

Donny cursed under his breath as I nodded. "That about sums it up."

The other tattooist came in. Tall and lean, he was covered in ink. Even his bald head had tattoos on it.

Silk looked over to him. "Hey, SeVen, shop empty?"

"Yeah, flipped the doorbell on in case anyone comes in. This about Gabs?"

Silk nodded to an empty spot at the table. "Yep, take a seat. We're about to get down to making some plans on how to prevent our girl from burning herself out completely."

He joined us at the table, and we spent the rest of the afternoon throwing around ideas between the three of them leaving to attend to clients. Not that we decided on much. Ultimately, Gabs needed to allow us in for us to help her.

There was one thing I could do without her direct help. It might be overstepping again, but hell, someone needed to do something before she ended up in hospital herself.

Chapter Fourteen

Boone

THE EASIEST WAY I could think of to take some pressure off Gabs was getting her landlord to step up. To do that, I headed over to the ranch with my SPCA partner, Logan, first thing the next morning.

"So, you know the owner?"

I shook my head as I pulled into the Emerson Ranch driveway.

"I know the woman who discovered the horses were being neglected. John Emerson is her landlord."

He whistled under his breath. "She ratted on her landlord? That's not gonna go over well."

"She didn't rat on him. She called me when she found the horses. She's taken on caring for them, on top of all her other responsibilities. I'm worried she's overdoing it."

"So, we're here to what? Take possession of the horses so she doesn't have to worry about them? Because, buddy, you know that's not how we normally handle these cases."

I clenched my jaw as I pulled up in front of the house, furious that Logan would even suspect me of unprofessionalism. I never had bent the rules, and I never would.

"I don't expect anything special out of this visit. I'm not out to break rules. We're here to check the animals' welfare and issue a warning if it's needed. I'm hoping we can get the Emersons to step up and look after their own damn animals. Just like any other case."

He frowned my way. "Settle down. I was just checking."

We got out and I knocked on the front door of the ranch house. It was early morning and I hoped they were home, not out working in a pasture, which would mean we'd have to go looking for them.

The door swung open, and I was greeted by a younger man who I guessed was Royce. He didn't look like a rancher. No bulk to his frame. He looked more like an accountant, one who would blow over in a stiff wind. But his clothes were dusty, as though he'd already been out doing ranch work.

Forcing myself to remain civil, I gave him the usual spiel we started with, pretending like I hadn't already guessed who he was. "Morning, sir. Are you John Emerson?"

He frowned. "He's in bed ill at the moment. I'm Royce Emerson, his son. What can I help you with?"

"We're from the SCPA and we've come to take a look at your animals."

His frown deepened as he ran his gaze up and down both of us before settling on my face. "Sounds like Gabriela's been stirring trouble. The woman does like to keep me on my toes."

He was the only one I'd ever heard call her by her full first name. Even her folks called her by her nickname. I raised an eyebrow at what he was implying but didn't say anything, letting my silence do its work.

"My folks came down sick a while back. I tried to keep up with everything but forgot about the horses. Gabriela has been helping me get them back to good. I think she's with them at the moment. We can head down there, if you want."

With a nod, I stood back and waited as he pulled on his boots. Logan and I followed him down to an ATV.

"It's a ways from the house. Want to follow me in your truck?"

"Sure."

Once we were in the truck, it didn't take long to get down to the barn. A few horses were out in the pasture. At a glance, I could see they were on the thin side, but they looked well-groomed and were happily nipping at the grass. The barn's main doors were open and as we walked in, Gabs stopped mid stroke to turn towards us. The gray mare she'd been brushing gave a snort and she shifted to pet and soothe her.

As my eyes adjusted to the dimmer interior, I could see the dark smudges under her eyes, the slump to her shoulders as she gave the horse some loving while frowning our way. She opened her mouth to say something, but Royce spoke before she could get a word out.

"As you can see, all the horses are being cared for." He moved over and rested a hand on Gabs' shoulder.

She stiffened and tried to duck out from under his grip, but the horse was blocking the only way she could take to escape the creep. I wasn't sure what to say. I wanted to pull her away from him and punch him in the face for touching what was mine, but I couldn't. I was here as a representative of the SPCA.

Logan cleared his throat and took over speaking with the asshole. My gaze was locked onto Gabs as she managed to get the horse to back up enough for her to slip around the front to the other side of the animal. She brushed down the mare's flank like she was simply continuing with what she'd been doing before we came in.

As Gabs finished up and moved to lead the horse out to the pasture, I tuned back into Logan and Royce's conversation.

"We'll be back in a month to check on how things are going with the horses," Logan said. "If you don't use them for ranch work anymore and have no time or interest in riding them for pleasure, it might be worth looking at selling them."

Hoping like hell the man listened and rehomed these beautiful creatures, I let Logan finish up then followed him back out to our vehicle to head off. I wished I could have gotten Gabs alone to talk to her but clearly that wasn't going to happen.

Once we were heading down the driveway, Logan spoke up. "He wants us to believe he's involved with Gabriela."

"Yeah, I caught that. The way Gabs talked about Royce led me to believe they weren't even friends. No way are they together."

The silence dragged before he spoke again. "She your girl then?"

I blew out a breath as I turned onto the

road back toward town. "I wish. We dated for a bit. Her life got turned on its head a couple months back when her folks were in a bad crash. I overstepped when trying to take care of her, and she pushed me away."

He nodded. "She looked in worse shape than the horses. I hope he listens and either steps up or sells them before she burns out and can't look after them or herself."

I prayed for the same damn thing, while wondering if I hadn't just overstepped again.

Gabs

Damn men. Always thinking they can just roll on in and fix everything.

"You called in the SPCA on me? What the fuck, Gabriela?" Royce all but growled.

I'd finished brushing down the last of the horses and they were all out in the pasture grazing now. I grabbed the fork and muck bucket then headed toward Whiskey's stall.

"I didn't call the SPCA. I've got no clue why they came out."

Turning so I could keep Royce in my line of sight, I started to sift the manure out of the bedding, dumping the horse shit into the bucket. He threw his hands up in the air.

"Well, how in the hell else could they have known?"

I rolled my eyes as I dumped the next fork full. "Gee, I don't know Royce. Maybe since your folks haven't been seen around town in months, one of their friends called it in. Don't be surprised if the cops rock up next to do a wellness check."

Maybe that was what I should do. Get the cops involved. Although, it would no doubt make Royce even harder to tolerate.

He paced over to the doorway that faced the pasture and mumbled under his breath.

"Maybe it'd be easier to just shoot them all." He shook his head. "Auction. Plenty of kill buyers there. Then I'll get some money out of it. Yeah."

My heart skipped a beat, and I nearly dropped the fork. I was well aware he was mean enough to shoot them just so people would leave him be. Selling such beautiful animals to the slaughterhouse wasn't any better. Emotions swelled, clogging my throat, and I couldn't take another moment in the monster's company.

Taking the fork and bucket out of Whiskey's stall, I set them down before marching over to Royce.

"Since you have so much free time, you can finish off the chores today. I'm leaving."

I was careful to stay out of his reach, not giving him time to respond before I headed to the door and into the pasture. As I stomped across the uneven ground, Whiskey and Flint shadowed me until I reached the fence near my trailer. With a huff, I turned to face them, reaching out to stroke down their noses.

"I'm sorry, girls. He just makes me so damn mad! I'll be back later to make sure y'all get bedded down with feed and water."

After another couple minutes of petting them, I climbed over the fence and headed inside to shower and change. As I washed off the morning's grime, I tried to think of how to prevent Royce from destroying the horses. Maybe I could ask around to see if anyone would want to privately buy them. Surely, they'd sell for more that way than whatever the kill buyers would offer.

If I could convince Royce he could earn more by privately selling the horses, I might be able to get him to agree to advertising them that way. Royce had always been all about the money. Hopefully, by the time I got back over there later, he'd have cooled off and be more reasonable to deal with.

Once more, concerns for John and Kate rose up. I still hadn't managed to get into the house to lay my eyes on them. The longer I went without seeing them, the more worried I got. Was Royce bastard enough to hurt his own parents? Parents who'd spoiled him rotten and given him everything he'd ever wanted.

I shook my head as I made my way through my trailer to the bathroom. I was just tired and letting my imagination run away with me. Maybe when I went over later, I'd try to sneak into the house to check on them. I'd been so busy with everything and trying to avoid Royce, who seemed to want to hit on me every chance he got, I hadn't even asked about John and Kate for a while now.

As I stripped then started the shower, my thoughts turned to Boone. He was about the only one I knew personally who had enough space for more horses, but I had no idea if he'd have the funds to buy them. Not that I'd be seeing him anytime soon to even ask. I was still furious about what he'd done. He'd taken my reaching out to him for advice and turned it over to his work with the SPCA. He'd broken my trust, and thanks to him poking around today, the horses could lose their lives. He should have just left well enough alone.

With a shake of my head, I recalled him pulling me away from the hospital, making it so I hadn't been there when my dad had taken a turn. What was with that man and interfering?

Damn cowboys. They were always trying to fix shit, even when they had no clue what they were doing.

With a sigh, I focused on getting showered and dressed as quickly as possible. I had way too much shit to do today to waste time here at home. As soon as I was ready, I grabbed my keys, phone, and handbag and was out the door.

First stop was the grocery store, which thankfully wasn't too crowded, so I could get everything I needed quickly before heading over to my parents.

I was putting things away when Mom came into the kitchen. I handed her a spoon and a single-serving tub of strawberry yogurt.

"Oh, my favorite. Thank you, Gabs."

She took a seat at the table and peeled off the lid. She was still moving slower than normal but other than that, she was looking good.

"How's your shoulder and arm feeling today?"

She took a mouthful of yogurt, humming a little as she enjoyed the treat before she responded.

"Almost back to normal. My shoulder aches if I lift things or use it too much, but that's getting less every day."

I continued emptying the shopping bags. "What about Dad? He up in bed?"

"Uh huh. Christopher's arranged for one of his friends to make home visits to get him started on some rehab exercises. He gave me some to do for my shoulder, too. Lovely man. He'll be here again tomorrow morning. Maybe you should come by a little earlier tomorrow? While he's here."

I barely resisted the urge to roll my eyes. "Mom, I don't need you to set me up with anyone, let alone my brother's friends."

"Well, if we want to see our grandkids before we're too old to enjoy them, I think I do."

I clenched my jaw until it ached as I finished putting the groceries away. It was an old argument, and this was far from the first time she'd attempted to set me up with someone.

"Why don't you take that up with Christopher then? He can provide you with grandbabies too, you know."

She waved a hand my way. "Pfft, he's way too busy working to fit in a family at the moment."

That one stung. Again, wasn't the first time I'd heard it from her mouth, but it never stopped hurting. It had been a long time since I'd bothered arguing with her about my job being real but today, I was at the end of my rope with everything that was going on. Something inside me snapped.

After putting away the empty bags, I spun toward my mother. "And you think I'm not? You think I have so much free time, I just what? Spend my days dancing through fields or something? I work hard, Mom. I've always worked my *ass* off. I don't have student loans, and you and Dad sure as shit never paid for any of my training like you did with Christopher, but I made it through an apprenticeship and helped Silk set up a new business. I own every damn thing in my trailer free and clear. I pay my own rent. And right now, I'd put money on the fact that it's me that's working harder than Christopher. When was the last time he came and actually helped out?" I waved her off as she went to speak. "I don't mean him coming over to sit with you and Dad, or send his friend over, but actually get some dirt under his nails and physically help. Did your shopping, cleaned your damn bathroom. Who does that every damn day? Me, that's who. I'm currently coming here every day to take care of you and Dad. I'm taking care of all the Emerson horses because John and Kate are ill, and Royce is fucking useless. On top of that, I'm still doing as many shifts at Silky Ink as I can because like I said, I've got rent to pay and food to buy. Because I *can,* and *do,* take care of *my fucking self!*"

Closing my eyes against the sting of tears, I blew out a breath before shaking my head.

"I'm done. I just can't do this today. You've got enough food for the rest of the week and you're well enough to help Dad with whatever he requires. I'm sure you'll figure out a way to get anything else you need."

Before Mom got over her shock, I grabbed my shit and rushed out the door. Wiping away the tears, I headed away from the house I'd grown up in and wondered if I'd ever go back. I never swore in front of my parents. Never called them out on their bullshit. I had no idea what the fallout would be from my outburst today, but I was sure there'd be some.

When I pulled into the parking lot behind Silky Ink, I grabbed my phone and turned it off before I headed inside. Whatever the fallout was going to be, it could wait till after I finished work.

Chapter Fifteen

Gabs

On autopilot, I nearly plowed into Donny as I rushed in through the rear entrance of Silky Ink.

"Whoa, Donny. What gives?"

He stood, arms folded over his broad chest, blocking the way to the front of the building.

"Done watching you destroy yourself, babe. I'd figured you'd have caved and let Silk in by now, but you haven't, so you got a choice. You either talk to me, SeVen or Silk. Your choice, but you will be going into the break room and we ain't letting you out till you fucking let at least one of us in and we have a plan in place to help you out of whatever the hell hole you've found yourself in."

Tears welled. After the altercation with my mom, I didn't have anything left to resist Donny's kindness.

"Don't we all have clients booked for tonight?"

He raised an eyebrow, letting me know he knew I was trying to get out of this intervention. "We'll cover for you and whoever you're most comfortable confiding in. You got thirty seconds to choose, or I'll pick for you."

Unable to hold my emotions back any longer, I sniffled before I wiped the tears from my cheeks.

"Silk. I'll talk to Silk."

"Excellent. Head into the break room. She's already in there waiting for you."

His gaze burned into my back until I closed the door behind me. Damn having caring workmates.

"Hey, doll. Come sit with me."

I sniffled again, blinking through the tears that I knew wouldn't stop now they'd started. "Intervention time, huh?"

She gave me a sad smile, "We all care about you, Gabs, and you have us all worried. This isn't like you."

I shook my head. "I've always been closed off."

"Not with me, you haven't."

I shrugged a shoulder as I moved to sit beside her on the couch. The moment my butt hit the cushion, she wrapped her arms around me and pulled me in for a hug, and I lost it. Burying my face in against her shoulder, I sobbed out everything.

"That's it, Gabs. Let it all out. I got you, girl."

I have no idea how long we sat like that, Silk stroking my hair and back while I drenched her shoulder with my tears. Eventually, the storm passed enough I could sit back and take a few breaths. I leaned over and snapped a couple tissues from the box on the side table and tried to mop up my face.

"Sorry about your shirt."

Silk laughed. "Babe, compared to what Raven smears all over me, tears are no problem." She grew serious. "Although, I hate you're this upset. Time to spill the beans."

I nodded then blew my nose. "Let me grab a drink."

Standing before she could offer to get it for me, I went and got a glass of water, downing half of it before I refilled and returned to sit beside Silk.

"I don't even know where to start, to be honest."

"How about why you went out to The Barn that night you met Boone? Normally you'd have come into Styx if you'd just wanted a drink."

Heat flashed over my cheeks. "I didn't want it to get back to you that I was out drowning my sorrows."

She sighed. "Not sure how I can get through to you that I'm still here for you, Gabs. I never went anywhere. Yeah, I got a man and baby now, but you're my best friend. Ain't nothing going to change that."

I took a drink before I answered. "Yeah. I know."

Damn, I really didn't want to admit my feelings about being jealous, so I cleared my throat and ignored that silent elephant in the room.

"Earlier that night, I'd been with the horses when Royce rolled in."

"Let me guess… he did his usual and tried to get into your panties? That boy needs to take a hint already."

She had no idea. I nodded. "When I shut him down, he got all butt-hurt over it and banned me from the property. Told me his dad was ill, so he was running everything. He wanted to kick me out of my trailer, but I spun him some bullshit about having a lease and he couldn't just throw me out because he wanted to. I still don't know what's going on with John and Kate. I haven't seen them, and

Royce won't let me into the house or answer my questions other than to say they're ill."

"That's some bullshit. We need to get the cops around there to do a welfare check, or we could get some of the club to do it."

That brought a smile to my lips. I could just imagine how Royce would handle a bunch of the Charon MC on his doorstep.

"Not sure, Silk. I was going to do that, but after I called Boone for some advice about the horses, he rocked up in his capacity as an inspector with the SPCA. Royce lost his shit, blaming me for ratting on him. Then he threatened to shoot the horses or send them to the slaughterhouse to solve the issue. That was today's drama."

Silk pulled me for another hug. "Oh, honey. No wonder you're so upset! I'm reading between the lines, but guessing once he banned you, no one looked after the horses?"

I left my head on her shoulder. "Uh huh."

"And that's what you were going to tell me when I didn't remember who Whiskey was. I do know who she is, you just haven't spoken to me about her for so long, it wasn't in the forefront of my mind."

I sat back up. "It's all right, Silk. I've been strung pretty tight lately and jumping on everyone." Which reminded me of my fight with Mom earlier. More tears leaked, and I mopped them up with another tissue, clearing my throat. "It'd been nearly a month since I was home for more than a few minutes. Whiskey was at the back fence when I did finally get there. She looked terrible. She was hurt too. She'd cut her chest breaking out of the barn."

"That why you called Boone? Because Whiskey was hurt."

I shook my head as I tossed the latest tissue into the trash. "Nah, I knew how to care for the wound." I huffed out a breath. "I guess, really, I used it as an excuse to call him because I missed him."

"What happened to make you break it off with him?"

"Him overstepping with the horses wasn't the first time he pulled that stunt. The day Dad had the embolism, Boone had dragged me away from the hospital and—"

Silk cut me off with a groan. "Please tell me you didn't blame him for you not being there when your dad took a turn?"

I shrugged a shoulder and looked at the opposite wall, focusing on the artwork Silk and I had done back when we'd first opened this place.

"Gabs, you have to realize it wasn't his fault. Or yours for not being there. Shit happens. I'm just grateful he was in the hospital when it did, so it got handled quickly."

I drank the rest of my water before I spoke again. "Maybe if I'd been there, I could have—"

"Stop right there, Gabs. At a guess, Boone saw you working yourself ragged and took you away for a day of relaxation and recharging. Yeah, the timing sucked with what happened with your dad, but he did it because he fucking cares! Not like he lured you away then went and smothered the man in his sleep. You need to forgive both you and him for that day. It wasn't anyone's fault."

Huffing out a breath, I glared at Silk for a minute. "Fine. It was no one's fault."

"Why don't you call him again, see if he can go out with you tomorrow night?"

I rolled my eyes. "Because I have to do the nightly chores at the barn then come in here to work."

She nudged my shoulder with hers. "I'm giving you the week off, paid leave. But I expect daily phone calls from you to check in, and if you need more time, you ask for it. Your name might not be on the damn sign, but you've worked as hard as I have to get this business up and running. Including never taking a damn vacation. You've earned some paid time off, although I wish it was because you were going somewhere nice."

I smiled over at my friend, grateful I hadn't lost her after all. "Okay, I'll give him a call."

Silk stood and headed to the door. "Head on home and call him. He can always help you with the horses, yeah? See if he can spend the day with you tomorrow after you've dealt with your folks."

Thankfully, she'd turned away from me and missed how I winced. We'd covered a lot tonight, but I hadn't told her about my fight with my mom or about the stunts I suspected Royce had pulled with my trailer. Maybe next time we chatted I'd fill her in on the rest.

Gabs

I waited until I got home before turning my phone back on. Before any messages could come through, I dialed Boone's number. When it went through to voice mail, I resisted the urge to hang up. Nerves had me pacing the length of my trailer as I waited for when I could leave my message.

"Hey, Bo. Silk's given me some time off

work, so I've got some free time this week. I'd love to see you. Call me."

I hung up and pocketed my phone. Ignoring the incoming pings of messages. I still wasn't ready to talk to Mom, or anyone in my family. Stopping by the kitchen window, I stared out toward where I knew the barn lay just out of view. I could go take Whiskey for a ride. It'd been so long since I'd gone for a relaxing ride. It would help settle my mind.

Chewing my lip, I contemplated if it was worth the risk of catching Royce at the barn. Although, it was probably fairly safe to assume he wouldn't be doing afternoon chores in with the horses. Hell, he probably hadn't finished the morning ones.

"Damn it."

I was going to have to go check on them regardless, so I might as well go now and get a ride in. If Silk was giving me the week off, I could cycle through all the horses, riding one each day to exercise them. They'd all love that.

Heading back to my room, I got changed into my riding gear, then headed off. There were still hours before the sun would set, so plenty of light for me to walk over. I was nearly at the barn when I heard voices come from within that had me stopping short.

"Helping you muck out stalls was never part of our agreement, Royce."

I remembered that voice. It was Billy, one of the men who'd attacked me at The Barn that night I'd met Boone.

"Well, if you want your cut, you need to do some of the damn work. You've played the part for long enough. Surely, you've picked up some cowboy skills along the way?"

What had Royce done?

Billy laughed. "We done learned all sorts of fun things, but only about the human kinda fillies, not the actual horse kind. Why the fuck are you out here doing this shit anyhow? Don't you got staff?"

Royce's anger was clear in his tone. "If I had a ranch hand, they'd notice what's going on up at the house don't you think? Gabriela was helping with the horses, but she stormed off earlier today after the fucking SPCA dropped in for a visit. I can't let the horses get any worse, or they'll be back and be a pain in my ass."

"Just sell them already."

Bob spoke for the first time. "Or shoot them."

"That was my first thought too, but they're worth too much to just kill 'em. As soon as I have enough time to put together their info, I'll get them advertised."

It was a small relief he wasn't going to kill them. I had no clue Royce even knew Billy or Bob. I'd never seen them around Bridgewater before and didn't think they were locals.

Billy spoke again, "This is all taking too long. This was supposed to be over in a month."

"You two are the idiots who went and got arrested. Be grateful I bailed you out and didn't just leave you there and find someone else."

Bob laughed again, the dark sound sending shivers down my spine. "You're the one who should be fucking grateful. How many men will help you off your folks so you can inherit a ranch you got no clue how to take care of?"

I stumbled back a step, my hand raising to cover my mouth, barely able to believe what I'd heard. I turned to head away, intending to stop and call the authorities as soon as I was sure I was out of earshot. But Whiskey chose that moment to come up to me. She whinnied a greeting and the moment she did, I knew I was fucked.

"Hey! Stop right there."

Needing to get away quickly, I rushed to Whiskey's side, grabbing her mane to help pull myself up onto her back. I rarely rode bareback, but I could do it. Before I could nudge her to take off, a gun went off and a flare of agony lit up my shoulder. The force of the blow knocked me from Whiskey, and I hit the ground hard enough to rattle my teeth. I tried to crawl away, but my body wouldn't move. Blackness crept into my vision, and it was all over.

Chapter Sixteen

Boone

RETURNING FROM EVENING CHORES, I went straight to the kitchen. Since my phone had gone dead, I'd left it plugged in when I headed out. I didn't like being out of contact for any length of time. Summer or the girls might need me.

Or maybe Gabs.

I shook my head, calling myself all sorts of stupid as I turned on my phone. As it dinged with a voicemail, the main radio in my kitchen I had set up to scan the local emergency channels cracked to life with news of a fire. Dialing into my voicemail, I kept half my focus on the call. Gabs' sweet voice filled my ear, asking me to call her, as the radio gave the address for the structure fire.

"Fuck!"

As far as I knew, Gabs' trailer was the only one anywhere near the Emerson's ranch. I prayed it wasn't her place, but my gut told me it was.

Hanging up from voicemail, I dialed her cell, praying she'd answer. It rang and rang until it flicked over to her recorded message. I didn't waste time with it. Hanging up, I grabbed my keys and sprinted out the front door to my truck. Once I was on the road, I didn't bother trying to call anyone for information, just put my foot to the floor to get to the location given over the radio as fast as I could.

With my heart in my throat, I pulled up away from the trucks and rushed over toward the trailer that was engulfed in flames. Anyone who'd been in there couldn't have survived. There would be nothing but rubble left when it was done.

Another car and three bikes pulled in next to my truck. Two older and one younger man wearing Charon MC colors got off the Harleys while Silk, Donny and SeVen came rushing over from the car.

Silk started talking before she reached me. "Please tell me you know where she is! I told her to call you. She should have been with you!"

A chill flashed through me as I shook my head. "I'd been hoping she was at work."

Tears tracked down her face. "I gave her the rest of the week off today. Told her to call you."

One of the older men who wore a name patch that said Bulldog pulled her into his chest. "We'll find her, Silky. She's too smart to have gotten caught inside."

Royce came out of somewhere and headed our way. Had the fucker been hiding and listening to us?

"Gabs was in there. She was helping me with the horses, but she came home about half hour ago."

That set Silk off into loud sobs, but something didn't sit right. I caught Donny's gaze, and he was clearly thinking the same thing. I tilted my head toward a couple of firefighters that had just grabbed bottles of water.

"Let's go see what we can find out."

Royce went to follow, but the other older biker, who's name badge read Scout moved to block him. "You stay right where you are."

Next to his name patch sat another one that said President. Gabs hadn't been kidding when she said she was under the protection of the club.

Donny spoke low as we walked the short

distance, "Don't trust that fucker. I know a few of the firefighters. Hopefully they'll give us some info."

I knew several of them too, from jobs involving animals. Between the two of us I was hoping we'd be able to find out something.

As we got closer, I could see their faces and was relieved to see Sid, who was around my age. We'd done several jobs together.

"Hey, Sid, can you tell me if anyone was in there?"

He finished drinking his bottle of water before he turned to look at Donny, the group behind us then back to me. "You know who lived here?"

I nodded, "My girl, Gab—"

Donny interrupted me, "Gabriela Rayne is her full name. I work with her down at Silky Ink. She wasn't at work, and she's not with her man. We're worried, man. If you could let us know if we should still be looking for her, that'd be great."

He was silent for a few moments before he nodded with a tight jaw. "Nothing will be official until the investigator is done. I don't wanna hear or see anything I say now comin' back at me, you hear?"

He should know me better than that, but I got why he felt the need to voice it. He'd be in deep shit if it was found out he'd released unconfirmed info early. "Not a word to anyone. I just wanna know if I need to keep looking for my girl, or if I gotta start grievin' her."

He looked me in the eye. "Keep looking. One of our guys was the first on scene. He was driving past when it first went up. He got a good look in the windows and called out. No response and he couldn't see anyone."

I clapped him on the shoulder. "Thanks, man. Let me know if you find out different."

"Will do."

With that, Donny and I rushed back to our little group. I rested a hand on Silk's back. "We need to keep looking for her."

I scanned around but didn't see Royce. "Where'd that bastard Royce go?"

The president nodded toward the pasture. "Said he had to go check on horses or some shit."

"I got a bad feeling he's behind this." I looked up and down the fence line until I spotted a gate. "Donny, go get the gate for me and we'll head over that way."

He jogged that direction while I went to my truck. As I shut the door, the younger biker climbed onto the bed and the opposite door opened as the club president climbed in. "Name's Scout, man on the back is Mac, and that girl is like a daughter to me. We'll handle whatever we find."

With a nod, I gunned the engine and headed toward the now open gate. I stopped long enough for Donny to join Mac in the bed, then I took off over the pasture, praying my girl was okay.

Gabs

With a groan, I woke up to agony. Fuck, what had happened?

"She's alive. Fuck. Dammit, I just lit her shit up to make it look like she died in her trailer."

"Another bullet will fix that."

"Don't you fucking dare shoot again. The fire is nearly out and there's a whole lot of people hanging around for news. Can't risk they'll hear it."

"Well, those fucking beasts won't budge for us, you go try to move them away from her."

"What happened to Bob?"

"Horse stomped him when he tried to get to the bitch."

The three of them kept talking but I tuned them out. They'd burned my house down?

Forcing my lids open, I blinked until I could make out that all three horses stood around me. We were close enough to the barn, there was enough light to see.

Whiskey stomped and neighed toward the men, clearly trying to scare them away from me. Damn, I loved these horses. They were literally saving my life right now.

An engine revved close and not wanting to risk moving and hurting myself more, I tried to see that way without turning my head. Was that Bo's truck with a couple men in the bed? I blinked away tears that kept coming and nearly sobbed when the truck skidded to a stop and Donny along with Mac from the Charons jumped down and took off after the men, Scout on their heels. Boone came toward me.

"Gabs? Sweetheart, tell me you're still breathin' darlin.'"

I could barely get a word out past the emotion clogging my throat, but I forced out his name. "Bo."

"Thank fuck. How we gonna get these girls to back off and let me at you?"

"I'm shot, and I fell hard. We need an ambulance."

He pulled his phone out and made a couple calls. Then lights flickered over the pasture and another car pulled up. Then Silk was there, with SeVen and Bulldog. Silk had come with me to visit the horses several times so they knew her. She came closer slowly.

"Hey, Whiskey, baby. You gonna let us get our girl some medical help?"

Boone had gone into the barn and returned with some treats to lure them away. Together with Silk, Boone got the horses to back up. Boone guided Silk and SeVen on what to do to get Whiskey, Cloud and Flint back into the barn where they bedded them down for the night. I looked around the best I could and saw that Bulldog had Bob pinned against the side of the building, but Scout, Mac and Donny hadn't returned yet.

Then Boone was dropping to his knees beside me. "Ambulance is nearly here. Fuck. I'm sorry I didn't answer your call. I'd left my phone at home… if I'd just—"

"Stop it. This was gonna happen at some point. Call another ambulance for John and Kate. Not sure if it'll be too late, but I heard them talking about how Billy and Bob had helped Royce off his folks so he could get the ranch.

Boone looked over at the man Bulldog held. "Is that the same guy from—"

"Yeah, the both of them." I cut him off before he could say more. The club didn't know about what had happened that night at The Barn, but Bulldog was no fool.

"Darlin', be straight with me right now. You've had trouble with these fuckers before today?"

Before I could come up with a way to soften the story, Bo spoke. "The night I met Gabs, we were at The Barn. She was in the back hallway with him and his buddy. They were trying to drag her out the back door."

"She broke my fuckin' nose!"

With a fist wrapped in his hair, Bulldog slammed his face into the wall, no doubt rebreaking his nose. "Now I have too. *Fucker*." He turned back to us. "I'm gonna go hold him around the other side. The club'll deal with him and his buddies."

I cleared my throat. "Thank you."

I hadn't wanted their help earlier, but clearly being charged for what they'd done hadn't done a damn thing to change their ways. They would continue to hurt people until they died. The club could arrange that and dispose of the bodies, so they were never found. I'd always chosen to ignore that side of the Charon MC but after today, I saw it in a different light. I'd sleep better in the future knowing for sure that my attackers were all gone from the world.

Chapter Seventeen

Boone

WATCHING Gabs being assessed then carefully loaded into the ambulance was something I'd never forget. She could feel her toes and fingers, which was a good sign, but her shoulders were a mess. She'd been shot in one and had landed on the other.

"She's a fighter. She'll pull through this."

I nodded but didn't turn to face Silk, who was with me in the waiting room. The ambulance had taken Gabs straight to Houston, since her injuries were so severe. Silk had jumped in my truck, and we'd followed the ambulance.

The door opened and I turned, thinking it was way too soon for news about Gabs but hopeful all the same. When Christopher came through with his mother, I turned away, not wanting to deal with them right then. Not that they took the hint.

"Boone? What are you doing here?"

I spun to glare at her brother. "I was the one who fucking found her. Where'd you think I'd be when my girl is in the hospital? Bigger question is, where were you when her house was burning down, and she was missing?"

This family did my head in. Silk rested her hand on my arm. "Why don't you go get a coffee or something? I'll fill them in. Maybe call your folks?"

I forced out a breath. "Thanks, Silk."

Then I hightailed it out of there before I said or did something that would no doubt get me kicked out of the hospital. It was a little surprising they'd bothered to come, to be honest. It seemed to me they all relied on her, but none of them even noticed when she needed help.

As I made my way down the hall, I pulled my phone out and dialed home.

"Hello?"

"Hey, Mom. Sorry to call so late. Gabs was in an accident at her landlord's barn and I'm at the hospital in Houston, waiting on her to come out of surgery."

"Oh, honey. That poor girl is having a time

of it, isn't she? You want us to come sit with you?"

My eyes stung at her instant support and compassion. "Ah, yeah. That'd be great. There are a few others here with me, but I'd love to have you here."

"Your father and I will be there shortly."

"Thanks. Ask to come through to the waiting room for Gabriela Rayne. If you have any trouble, call me. Her brother works here, so I'll get him to pull strings if I have to."

After hanging up, I went and got a bottle of water. I was edgy enough without adding coffee to the mix. By the time I returned to the private waiting room, Gabs' family was sitting together, and Silk was pacing. Choosing a seat several away from them, I sat back and took a swig out of my water. My eyes slid shut, but I forced them open when all I saw was Gabs covered in blood, laying broken in the grass, her horses guarding her.

Silk's phone buzzed and she took it out, read something, then came to sit beside me.

"What's the news?"

"They found John and Kate up at the house. They're both alive but in comas. It's not looking good. They found poison in the kitchen."

"Did Scout and Donny catch Royce and Bill?"

"It'd have been in that last text if there was still a hunt going on, so I'm guessing they did."

I shook my head. "It's ballsy to be texting any of that shit, ain't it?"

"Nah, the club uses an encrypted program for this stuff. What happened with Bill and Bob before today?"

I turned to look her way. "Gabs would have told you if she'd wanted you to know."

Tears tracked down her cheeks. "We had a big chat earlier today. I thought she'd told me all she'd been holding back, but I guess she skipped some stuff. Please tell me."

I blew out a breath. Figuring it'd come out anyhow, I decided I might as well tell her.

"I first met Gabs when she was standing in a hallway with them. She'd broken Bob's nose, and was antagonizing Billy into attacking her. She had her fists up like she could take him on. I doubt it would have ended well for her had Jack, Liam and I not gone to her rescue." I shook my head. "She took a couple hits, but nothing some ice and Advil didn't fix. She had them charged. A couple deputies came and took them in."

Silk nodded. "She's never liked how the club deals with this shit. Be interesting to see if she changes her mind now."

I took another drink of my water. "I'm

struggling to accept it myself, but the fact Gabs is now safe is making it easier to understand."

"Yeah, they know how to solve a problem."

I tilted my head toward Gabs' family. "They always been like that with her? Putting her last?"

She sighed. "Yeah. They don't think her job is a real one. Like she didn't work her ass off to be where she is. Doesn't help her brother's a fucking plastic surgeon. I've never liked how her folks are with her. I ran interference a bit when we lived together..." She paused to wipe her eyes. "She has good reason to think I've backed away from her. It wasn't on purpose. Babies have a way of taking all your time without you fully realizing it."

"Where is your little one?"

"Eagle's on daddy duty at the moment. In the morning, he'll either come in with him, or he'll drop him at my Aunt Rose's then come in. Everyone in the club loves Gabs. She's not been coming to the barbecues and family functions lately. I've been fielding questions for a while about where she's at."

Unsure what else to say, I stayed quiet as we waited for news on Gabs.

Gabs

For the second time today, I woke to pain but at least this time I was on a bed, not the ground.

"You coming back to us, Gabs? C'mon, sweetheart, open your eyes."

Boone's deep voice had me forcing my lids open. I smiled when I saw he was real and not a dream. I tried to reach for him but quickly realized moving my arms wasn't going to happen.

"Don't try to move. You dislocated your right shoulder when you landed on it and your left took a bullet. It didn't hit anything vital and missed the bone. A through and through. But it's gonna hurt like a bitch for a while. Thankfully, your spine is all good. Guess you can thank your shoulder for taking the hit."

Relief had me closing my eyes for a moment. I'd been so scared when I'd woken up from falling. The pain in my shoulders eclipsed the rest of my body so I couldn't really tell what else was injured.

"They kept you sedated through the night, so you'd rest."

I nodded and scanned the room, looking for anyone else.

"Silk's just gone to the cafeteria with Eagle and Raven, but she'll be back any minute. And Christopher took your mom home last night once you were out of surgery and we knew you wouldn't be waking up till today."

"Okay."

What else could I say? I'd not left the hospital until I was forced to when Mom and Dad were here, but I didn't get the same in return. I did understand they were both still healing, but it still stung.

"I guess you'll need to get going back to the ranch...."

My voice trailed off as I stared down at the white bedding, unsure what I was even asking.

"My father and Liam have the ranch covered. They're also looking in on the Emerson place."

That had me looking up at him. The moment my gaze locked with his, he gave me a small smile. "Gabs, I ain't leaving you, darlin'. I get you're not used to being someone's top priority, but that's what you are to me. What you'll always be. I'm gonna always choose you. Always be here for you. All you gotta do is let me."

Tears welled and I bit my lip when it started to tremble. His expression softened, and he leaned in to wipe the moisture from my cheeks. Standing, he moved to press a soft kiss to my lips, and I moaned as I returned the kiss. His lips were warm and soft, and I wanted more. More than my body was ready for.

With a groan, Boone pulled back. "Damn, it's gonna be hard to wait until your shoulders are all healed up. Been missing you, Gabs."

I sniffled then cleared my throat. "Well, with both shoulders screwed up, my calendar just freed right up." I stopped short when I inhaled and caught a faint scent of smoke from Boone. "Last night, Royce said something about burning my shit."

The way Boone winced had me bracing for bad news. "Sorry, Gabs. Your trailer's gone."

Shock hit me. Everything I owned was gone. "Where am I gonna live?"

"That's up to you. I'd love for you to come stay with me, at least while you're healing. You can have the spare bedroom, there's no pressure for anything. I just worry if you move back with your folks, they'll have you helping out around the house way before you should be. I believe Silk also offered, and Scout mentioned the clubhouse."

I chuckled at that thought. "The

clubhouse has an upper level that's like hotel rooms. Some of the brothers and prospects live there. Trust me, I do not want to try to recover there. And you're probably right about my folks." I sighed. Moving in with Silk would be nice, like old times, but she did have a baby to care for now. "I need to think on it. This thing between us is so new, I don't want to wreck it by moving too fast, you know?"

He nodded but I didn't miss the hurt in his gaze.

"I'm not rejecting you, Bo. I promise. I'm so sorry I pushed you away after my folks' accident. I panicked and made some shitty choices. I won't be repeating those mistakes. I like you a whole helluva lot, and I don't want to rush in and ruin things this time around."

"Knock, knock!"

Silk came in, Raven in her arms and Eagle behind her. "Oh, you're awake!" She turned and thrust her son at her husband before she rushed over. I tensed, but she skidded to a stop before she hit the bed. "Damn it. I can't even hug you!"

"Yeah, sorry. Can't even hold Bo's hand at the moment."

She winced. "No way you'll be working anytime soon, either. Guess this is one way to get you to take it easy, but in the future, I'd prefer if you just took a vacation like a normal person, right?"

Chuckling, I shook my head. "I'll keep that in mind."

"Has anyone gone in to check on John and Kate?"

Her expression went serious. "I dropped in to check on them on my way here. They were both found unconscious in their bed. I overheard the nurses talking, and it's not looking good for Kate. I'm sorry. John is apparently showing signs he will wake up soon. Guess Royce was dosing them the same amount of poison and since John's bigger, it didn't affect him as much."

That had me frowning. "I don't understand why he didn't just kill them outright if that's what he wanted. Why make them suffer?"

Eagle spoke up, "At a guess, he was hoping the poison would bring on something natural like a stroke or heart attack that he could be blameless for. Club's looking into it. He had a pretty big life insurance policy on both of them."

I couldn't understand how anyone would do such a thing. Taking any life for momentary gain was horrible, but to kill your own parents who never did anything but love you? That was inconceivable.

"Right, well, on a lighter note! Have you decided on where you want to go when you break free of this place? Because I'd love to have you with us. You'll get all the baby cuddles you need — once your shoulders heal enough to accept them."

Looked like I wasn't going to have long to decide what I where I wanted to go, after all.

Epilogue

Three Months Later

Gabs

Moving in with Silk had been the right
decision. It had meant lots of time to catch up
and chat about everything that had happened
in both our lives. My left shoulder had healed
up fast enough I could head into Silky Ink
after just a few weeks, although the others
didn't let me do anything but the front
counter and only if I sat while I did it.

"You ready to get free of that thing?"

I smiled over at Silk, who'd driven me to
my doctor's appointment. "So ready!"

Tears threatened as I took in my best
friend. She was glowing, happy with her life. I
can't believe I nearly let it all fall away. Silk

parked but I didn't reach for the door right away. "Silk?"

She turned with one hand on her door handle, "Yeah, babe?"

"Thank you for not giving up on our friendship, even when I sorta did."

Her expression softened as she sighed. "Gabs, we both let it slide. I had a crazy year being kidnapped by the mob, dealing with my dad's seedy past, then hooking up with Eagle and getting pregnant. But that's just it… we've been friends for so long, we can have quiet times but know I'll always be here for you. No matter what is going on in my life, you can call on me, yeah?"

I smiled broadly at her. "Yeah, I get that now. Love you like a sister, Silk."

"Right back at ya. Now let's go get your arm free!"

With a chuckle, I slid out of the car and led the way to the doctor's office.

Since both Silk and Boone, along with Donny and SeVen, had made sure I'd taken it extremely easy as I recovered, the doctor was happy with my scans and took the brace off me. He told me I'd still need to be careful about over-extending the joint, and recommended I start seeing a physiotherapist to rehab both my shoulders. Something I'd already planned on doing. I wanted to ride and work with horses and needed full mobility in my shoulders. I refused to allow Royce to take that from me.

Before long, I was back in Silk's car, and we were heading out of Houston. After a stop at a Sonic to feed my addiction with a large Vanilla Coke. As we got closer to Bridgewater, Silk turned off the highway.

"Ah, Silk, whatcha' up to?"

"Got a surprise for you. Just sit tight and you'll find out soon enough."

The further down the road we got, the more worried I became, because she was heading toward my old place. I hadn't been back since the fire. I'd spoken to John on the phone when he'd called to apologize and confirm there was nothing left of my trailer to salvage. My car had been parked far enough away from the trailer that it had avoided getting burned, although I had no keys. Scout had fixed that one for me and my car was now sitting at the Charon MC clubhouse, safely locked away until I could drive it again.

"Silk, I don't want to see it."

Hearing the panic in my voice, she reached over and patted my leg. "We're not going to your trailer. Promise."

Then she turned up the main drive to the Emerson property. I stayed quiet but frowned as we passed the house and headed toward the barn. My heart hurt with how much I missed Whiskey, Cloud and Flint, but I could hardly drive myself out here and if I did get someone to bring me, I couldn't go for a ride or work with them at all, so I hadn't bothered.

"What have you two done now?"

Boone stood leaning against his truck that had a horse trailer attached to the back. John was beside him and they'd obviously been deep in conversation before we'd pulled up.

"It was John's idea. We just suggested the timing. Go and say hi to the horses, I hear they've missed you."

Fighting tears already, I slipped out of the car and cradling my right arm against my tummy, started toward the men. Boone straightened and came to meet me.

"You got the doc's approval to lose the brace. That's great."

He gave me a quick peck on the lips but before I could ask him anything, he had me turned and heading toward John. The man had aged twenty years since I'd last seen him. As far as he knew, Royce was still missing, although he'd lived in Bridgewater long enough to know the Charons had handled him and his two friends. Despite what the nurses had said, Kate had woken from the coma, but she wasn't the same woman. She was now living at an assisted living facility in Houston.

"Afternoon, Gabs. You're looking better. I can't apologize enough—"

I waved my left hand, cutting off his words. "You were more a victim than me, John. There's no need to apologize. Although, I am curious why we're all out here."

"Well, I'm selling the place. With Kate in the city, I want to be closer to her, not out here chasing cattle. I've lined up a buyer for the ranch, but I didn't sell him the horses. I wanted to gift them to you. I wasn't sure you'd be able to take them until I spoke with Boone here, and he assured me he has the stalls available and you're welcome there anytime you want."

Shock had me silent for a minute as I processed what John was saying.

"Are you sure? You could get a lot of money for them."

He smiled sadly. "The sale gave me more than enough to buy a small place near Kate. She's all I have left. You love those horses and I know you'll care for them. It's also been obvious these past months they're pining for you. It would be cruel to keep you separated permanently."

I swiped the tears from my cheeks. "They

saved my life. They blocked them from getting to me after I fell from Whiskey."

He nodded. "Yeah, I read the reports and spoke with Scout. You're bonded, especially to Whiskey, so I'm giving them to you."

"Thank you. I will cherish all three of them for the rest of their lives."

With a final nod and grim smile, he turned and walked back toward the house.

"I don't even know how to process what just happened."

"How about you go in and say hi to them for a start, then Silk will help us load them up and we'll get them over to my place."

Giddy with excitement, I rushed into the barn and was greeted by three loud whinnies.

"Hello, ladies, I've missed you too!"

Starting with Whiskey, I went to each one and gave them some pats, rubs and cuddles.

"Guess we're taking you to your new home now!"

Boone didn't want me risking hurting my arm, but Whiskey refused to budge for him or Silk, so using my left hand to hold her lead, I guided her out to the trailer. Once all three were loaded, I turned to Boone and threw myself into his arms. He caught me with a laugh and spun me around before putting me back down.

"Right. Well, I think that's my cue to leave! Have fun, kids!"

I waved over Boone's shoulder to Silk as she got in her car and headed off.

"Guess that means you're stuck with me and the horses."

He lowered his head and kissed me, not stopping until he had me dizzy with desire.

"Gabs, I love you to the moon and back, darlin' and I'll gladly be stuck with you forever."

Tears tracked down my cheeks again as joy blasted through my heart.

"I love you so much, Bo. Let's get the horses settled so I can show you just how much I've missed your touch."

"That sounds like the perfect plan."

The End.

More Silky Ink books are coming! Donny and SeVen will get their stories told real soon.

For all the links and information, head over to www.khloewren.com